The Last Responder

MATT SIMONS

Table of Contents

PROLOGUE

"WHAT DO YOU MEAN YOU can't make the gig to-morrow Sebastian?" Ben asked, gripping his bass more like a bat than musical instrument.

I say, "Exactly, what I said. I told you not to book anything this weekend last month. This whole weekend is for the police academy entrance requirements. I have the written exam in an hour. Then the physical fitness test tomorrow morning. Followed up by in person interviews Sunday. And I don't want to mess that up again with a late-night show."

"If you bail, you will kill all the momentum we've gained!" Ben gestures to the rest of the band. "Come guys back me up here."

Nicolas and Lilith are having their own aggravated conversation behind Nicolas's drum kit regarding their relationship. Ben snaps his fingers a few times trying to get their attention, "Guys!"

Nicolas doesn't look at Ben only lifting his finger to indicated one moment. Keeping his attention on Lilith. "I already told you. I don't know how she got my number or why she sent me those pics."

Lilith holding Nicolas's phone out. "You are unbelievable, you know that!" Ready to smash the device at any moment. "How could you let another women sext you… you… unbelievable bastard!"

I say, "Listen Ben. I've dedicated my whole life for this. I finish my degree in two months. I'm going to become a police officer just like my grandfather. I can't risk failing another round of preliminaries because you want to get crossfaded at a bar while playing music."

"This is a betrayal to the fans. You know that, right?" Really pouring on the guilt.

Annoyed by his attitude I finally snap, "What fans? Our fans are my parents, sometimes. And whomever is at the bar when we play. Which last time was just the bartender until he went out for a smoke break."

Ben rolls his eyes, "You just don't know how to sacrifice for the music."

"Sacrifice? I don't know what sacrifice is. How dare you say that to me!" Rising my voice for the first time to my childhood friend. "I had to leave my neighbors band for you. Walt was the man that taught me how to play guitar. And I left those old guys because I had to get a job to pay for this jam space." I gesture to the basement room as a cockroach scurries from one hole in the wall to another. "You haven't paid rent on this place once yet. Despite the fact you're always down here getting high. While I bust my ass serving ice cream to angry people, while I break myself to get my criminal justice degree as my student loans compile more debt. And you know what?"

Ben asks, "What?" glaring at me.

Lilith yells, "Fuck you! It's over!" as she throws Nicolas's phone at the wall. Leaving a new hole in the dry wall.

I say, "My thoughts exactly." Packing up my guitar and my amp before walking away.

Ben yells at me as I drag my stuff down the long narrow hall of the former office turned jam space. "Fine than! I don't need you to make it anyway."

While Lilith and Nicolas continue their breakup behind him.

That was five years ago.

CHAPTER 1
MORGUE RUN

"JUST ONE MORE DAY," I mumble, chewing dry spaghetti noodles for breakfast.

I'll get paid tomorrow, then I can go grocery shopping. I'll even be able to do laundry, thankfully, because my scrubs are getting gross. Fortunately, everything in the hospital smells kind of foul.

The sun is just starting to rise over the largest single-story hospital in the United States. Part of the land agreement about seventy years ago was that the builders could not obscure the view of the mountains for the local residents, so instead of building up, they'd had to build out. The hospital's property spans a total of nine square miles. When all the original residents finally died the hospital built its famous surgery tower. That casts a long shadow over me. This used to be an intimidating view from the fourth floor of the parking garage that's technically not part of the hospital's land. I did watch my grandfather pass here when I was a kid. Now after a year of working the endless halls, this place has just become a mundane part of life.

It's a three-hundred-yard walk to clock in. I pass many other scrub wearers as we collectively move to the hospital.

Nurses in plan blue scrubs, nurse technicians in light blue scrubs, green scrubs for the surgical staff, black scrubs for the equipment technicians, and then there's me in the navy-blue scrubs of the transporters. At least that's what everyone tells me my color is. I think it looks purple. But if I had perfect vision, I would not be doing this for a living.

Making my way into the building, I hold the door open to everyone else coming in for shift change. No one thanks me. One nurse kind of grunts as she drinks her coffee. Everyone just grabs a fresh cloth mask out of a box, per hospital policy that everyone wears one.

The Transportation Department is next to the loading docks for the cafeteria. The office's perimeter is lined with broken beds and stretchers. Makes me think of an industrial garage for hospital equipment.

I greet everyone with a "Good Morning. How's everyone today?" as I clock in with my badge.

I'm met with exhausted grunts and one person saying, "I'm here, aren't I."

My equipment consists of a Vocera, which is essentially a hospital-wide radio assigned to an individual, and a work phone that notifies me of my assignments such as where a patient is and where I need to take them. I also grab an extra set of large gloves and three pens. Nurses are notorious for stealing my pens.

My manager, Mrs. Fall, is the only one in a good mood. "Good morning, Sebastian. There's a morgue run waiting for you."

The job lights up on my work phone. *Patient: Male, age 78, weight 256 lb, height 6 ft 6 in, ICU room 401.*

"Am I going to have help with this one?"

"Rich should be getting the cart now."

I say, "A heck of a way to start the morning," as I begin my journey up hill to the ICU.

A short man who recently celebrated his sixtieth birthday, Rich has been working as a transporter for nearly forty years. I find him in the patient's room, with the nurse signing the paperwork to release deceased into our care.

I greet them both, "Good morning."

The nurse says, "Not to me. This is the end of my shift. I just need to give a report to the morning nurse and then I'm out for the next three days." She leaves me and Rich alone with the deceased patient.

Looking at the patient and the cart, I say, "I don't think he's going to fit."

We use a special cart for morgue runs. It's a six-foot-long metal cart with a removable steel frame for a tarp cover to hide the blue body bag.

Rich says, "Probably not, but we can't take him in the bed."

We lock the bed next to the cart, and Rich pulls while I push with all my might. We manage to move the patient partly into the cart. With a reposition, we try again. After an excessive amount of grunting and sweating, we get the large patient into the cart and then have to bunch him up so we can get the steel frame over and close the covering tarp. Thankfully rigor mortis hasn't set in yet.

There is only one rule for morgue runs, which is to never go past the cafeteria. However, the only other way takes us past the café. It doesn't help that the cart looks similar to the buffet carts.

As I push the cart to the morgue, I say, "I hate this season."

Agreeing with a nod, Rich says, "Yeah, all the snowbirds come to Arizona to die."

"We need real heat to burn them out."

"I'm good waiting on the heat for bit longer."

The morgue is next to the lab and across from the gym, down a long hallway with no natural light. The dreaded Buck Hall. The clean white walls with bright light 24/7 give this passageway an eerie, out of time feeling. The morgue is not labeled, just has a staff only sign. Inside there is a forklift on the wall next to a walk-in freezer, which is pad-locked, and the key is kept in a nearby drawer. The freezer only stores eight bodies on metal carts stacked two high. Today there are six already on the cold metal carts, so now we have to play a game of Tetris to get an empty cart out, moving carts out of the freezer, reshuffling everything, until we can use the forklift to move the body onto a freezer cart. I hate how dim the lights are in this room.

After the freezer is relocked, Rich takes the paperwork next door to Pathology at the end of the lab while I clean the transport cart with bleach wipes. Then I ball up the wipe into my glove as I strip it off and then sling shot it into to the trash. I'm becoming a pretty good shot with that.

When Rich gets back, we mark the job as complete on our phones only to have another morgue run pop up.

"Well, at least this guy weighs less than a hundred pounds," I quip.

Rich points out, "And we already made an open slot in the fridge."

While we go back to the ICU, Rich talks about his plans for Valentine's Day, how he's going to spend three days with his wife in Flagstaff. They're both big music fans there is a massive folk, blues and bluegrass festival featur-ing talent from across the country. It's a tradition that they have done for years. Then he asks, "What about you?"

"Probably just work same as today."

"Just work? You gotta have more than just this. Otherwise, this place will grind you up. I've seen many a fresh-faced kid get beaten down by this place."

"I'm not some kid and this is the best job I've ever had. I spent last year cleaning pools for a living. Here I get to work inside during the hottest and the coldest times of the year. Plus, I'm not getting attacked by angry dogs protecting their yard."

We enter the ICU where we hear the sounds of a patient yelling incoherently at a group of nurses trying to administer care.

Rich says, "Well, here you have to worry about patients taking a swing at you. How good's your dodge?"

I pretend to evade an imaginary punch. "Good enough. I ain't been hit yet."

We have to wait for the irate patient to calm down before we can get a nurse to sign off on the latest dead body.

This time when I grab the bag, I realize why they weigh less than a hundred pounds. "This one ain't got no legs."

CHAPTER 2
SHIFT CHANGE

I HATE THE BEGINNING OF THE shift because 7:00 a.m. is a chaotic mess. All the night nurses want to leave and are trying to give reports to the day nurses while at the same time all the different testing units and surgery rooms open and want their patients, putting the transporters in quite a pressured situation.

My first job after the morgue run is to take a patient from the Cardiac Care Unit at the farthest south side of the hospital to Nuclear Medicine at the northern most end of the hospital. At least they're under three hundred pounds, but they are eighty-five years old and will probably have a hard time transferring from their bed to my stretcher.

As soon as I walk onto the unit, I am bombarded with the sound of loud beeping alarms from empty IVs as nurses are busy either getting a report or trying to find the nurse to get a report from.

After getting my paper printed, I go to the secretary at the desk in the center of the unit. "Good morning, do you know who is currently in charge of room 655, bed two?"

The secretary is a young woman, though her face is mostly covered with a mask like everyone else so it's hard to guess her age, maybe about twenty. Her thick, dark curly hair is starting to stick out of her cap. Annoyed by my presence, she keeps her focus on her computer screen as she says, "Can't you read the chart? It has everyone's assigned rooms."

"I can, but has the night nurse left yet or is it still technically their patent?"

Still not looking at me, she says, "I don't know. Go figure it out."

I have to remind myself to not be an asshole this early in the morning, it's all just a job, so I say as nicely as I can muster, "Thank you." The nice thing about always wearing a mask is that I never have to fake a smile.

I find the day nurse as she's about to go into a patent's room with several other nurses, and I ask her, "Have you gotten report for room 655, bed two? I need to take them to Nuc Med."

Franticly, she says, "No, I haven't even seen the night nurse yet. I have no clue what's happening with them."

"Okay, well… I'm going to take them for a test, I guess. Whenever I find the night nurse."

I walk up and down each of the four long hallways of the 650s Unit asking for the night nurse. Night shift never bothers to have a Vocera on them. Eventually I come upon a cutout in one of the hallways where four nurses are working on computers and laughing about something.

I interrupt their laugh to ask, "Are any of you in charge of 655, bed two?"

Three of the nurses turn to the fourth nurse on the end as she says, "Yes! Are you taking them for the stress test?"

"I guess. My orders are to get them to Nuc Med. I have no other information." I hand her the paperwork to sign.

She scribbles on it and hands it back to me.

I thank her, then start to leave but stop when I see the illegible markings she used to sign with. Turning back to her, I say, "I'm sorry, but you didn't sign this correctly. I need your employee numbers, not your personal signature."

Still cheerful, she says, "Oh, I never give that. I don't trust anyone with it."

I say, "You must be a travel nurse. That's okay, but this hospital's policy is to sign with your employee numbers so the paperwork can be traced back to you. Anyone could just scribble a signature. And if something were to happen to the patient in transport, you could deny that you gave me permission to take the patient. I don't want to be held liable." I hand the paper back to her.

She doesn't take it.

I'm thinking, *Please don't make me be mean to you. You're the first person today who has been remotely nice to me.*

Then she says, "No, I don't want to give you my numbers."

Damn it. "Alright, then I can't take the patient."

Her cheer disappears and she yells at me, "You need to take him! He needs this test. I've been waiting all night for you slow pokes to come get him!"

It takes all of my control to not yell back. "I can't take a patient without proper paperwork. Otherwise, I will lose my job."

I will not go back to cleaning pools in the Arizona summer. I was attacked by way too many customers' dogs, poisonous wildlife, and one gnarly alley cat. I look to the other nurses to back me up, but none of them say a word and have unreadable faces under their masks.

With a sigh, I try one last time. "Please just give me your employee number."

She says with defiance, "No!"

Defeated, I say, "Fine." Then I speak into my Vocera, "Call Transportation," as I begin to leave the unit.

She calls me an asshole as I leave.

Transportation dispatch answers, "What's up, Sebastian?"

I reply, "Cancel my job. The night nurse is refusing to give her employee number on the paperwork."

"Really?"

I toss the paperwork into the trash as I leave the unit. "Yeah, the nurse doesn't trust anybody to have her number."

Dispatch says, "Alright, I'll tell Nuc Med."

I say, "And pass it on to Rod. This has been happening too frequently with the new travel nurses. Maybe the big boss man can make sure the policies are properly explained to them."

"You got it. The job has been canceled. Could you come back to dispatch real quick? We need you to train the newbie."

"Sure." Looks like another poor unfortunate soul has decided to work here.

CHAPTER 3
THE TRAINEE

A S I GET BACK TO dispatch, I take a moment outside the door to crack my neck and settle my mind. The last person I trained didn't last the day. They were overweight and couldn't handle the walking this place requires. Transporters walk an average of nine to twelve miles a shift while pushing weight. Plus, because the architect of this place was evil, there are hills to navigate. The Radiology Department sits at the top of a hill at the center of the hospital, and one must pass it to get to any other department. I swear if I ever meet that diabolical bastard, I will kick them in the shins with spiked cleats and force them to push beds up and down that infernal hill until they die.

I enter transportation dispatch and take off my mask for some fresh air. The dispatcher, Alfred, is talking to another transporter on the phone. He just points to the break room next to the bathroom. Entering, I see there is only one person sitting at the break room table, looking at their phone.

"Are you the trainee?"

She quickly puts her phone away before turning to greet me. A beautiful young woman with long blonde hair pulled back into a ponytail, she gives me an enthusiastic smile and says, "I'm Emily."

"Sebastian. Welcome to the grind." I should be enamored by how gorgeous she is, but my first thought is that this place is going to crush her.

My phone lights up with a job, so I tell her, "Come on, I'll show you the ropes."

We leave dispatch, and Emily walks next to me but slightly slower, not knowing where anything is yet.

"This is the main hallway, where the majority of rooms are. Starting with Unit 900, going all the way to Unit 600, one side is all hundreds and the opposite side is the 50s."

As we pass the 800 Unit, we hear an old woman screaming incoherently. Emily freezes after almost going toward the sound.

I guess now is as good of a time as any to explain the truth of this place. "That's not our current job." And I begin walking again, persuading her to follow.

She quickly catches up.

"Emily, why do you want to work in a hospital?"

It takes a moment before she realizes I said anything. "Oh, I love the show *Grey's Anatomy* and it inspired me to want to work in the medical field."

I keep us walking toward the job in the 750s Unit. "I'm sorry to burst your bubble, but hospital work is nothing like TV. First of all, you will maybe see a doctor once in a blue moon. We primarily deal with nurses, and almost all of them are in a bad mood. In fact, most people here are in a bad mood. No one wants to be in a hospital because being here means something went wrong and now they're suffering, sometimes dying." We reach the unit. "We transporters can't do very much to help. We are not allowed to give patients any form of medication and we have to be careful if they ask for food or water because there's a good chance that they're NPO, meaning nothing by mouth. So we can't give them any water no matter how much the patient pleads. All we can do is provide CPR in an emergency but there are far more experienced nurses for that." We reach the front desk and print up the paperwork. "Also, as an extra heads up because no one warned me when I first got here, but you will see a lot of gross stuff. Old men do not like to wear pants."

CHAPTER 4

PEACH

THE CURRENT JOB IS TO take a patient to dialysis, so I tell my trainee, "The Dialysis Department likes to fill up their bays as soon as they open in the morning, putting in all their jobs in at once. Then in a few hours, they'll switch them out. The other part that makes dialysis jobs hard is the fact that the patient has to go in their bed instead of the much lighter stretchers that line the primary hallway. Although, the nice part is that we won't have to transfer them from the bed to the stretcher."

"There's a list at the front desk of every unit, with the nurses' names and their room assignments. However, the nurse overseeing my patient has a name I can't exactly pronounce correctly into my Vocera, the microphone is very particular on pronunciations." So I ask the secretary while trying my best to not butcher the name too badly, if they have seen the nurse I need.

The secretary says nothing, only pointing behind me to a nurse on a computer at a nearby desk.

"Thank you." I try to smile but then stop after remembering my mask hides my face.

The poor nurse is holding her forehead in her hands, while staring at the computer screen.

I speak softly so as not to scare her, "Hello, we're here for your patient in 761 to go to dialysis."

Letting out a breath of relief, the nurse says, "Thank god." She then signs my paperwork correctly. "Be careful, he's a real peach."

"Oh, no…that bad?"

She nods her head, eyes wide to emphasize the problem I just inherited.

Emily asks, "Peach?"

I reply, "We refer to a particularly difficult patient as a peach because we can't outright call them a motherfucking asshole."

Emily's eyes widen and her jaw drops open slightly.

"Not something they show on TV. Now, I want you to remember that this guy is probably going to say a lot of really mean things. Don't take it personally. They're just looking for someone to yell at. Remember, it's just a job."

The nurse chimes in, "He is on oxygen, so you'll need a tank."

"Actually, could you show Emily where those are while I prep the patient for travel?" There is a need to protect this girl from the nightmares of this place. I don't want her first experience to be getting yelled at.

They walk away, and I take a deep breath. "Here we go." I knock and open the door. "Hello, I'm Sebastian with Transportation. I'm here to take you to dialysis." A phrase I have said hundreds of times, it feels robotic as it leaves my mouth. I have to make a conscious effort to not say it as I enter my own home.

The patient answers me with, "It's about fucking time, dipshit! All of you morons are too damn slow!"

He continues to ramble off complaints, curses, and a few racial slurs as I begin adjusting his bed for transport. I raise the side rails to keep the patient from rolling out of the bed, then I raise the bed to a comfortable height for pushing it. I'm fairly tall and don't want to hurt my back. Then I unplug the bed's power.

"Alright, we are all set. I just need a tank of oxygen and then we can go."

The patient growls, "I ordered breakfast. I ain't going nowhere until I get it, you fucking moron. Didn't they tell you that?"

Maintaining my calm. "I was not informed about that. They will probably just deliver it to you in dialysis."

"Probably?! What kind of answer is that? You don't know anything. Who lets a fucking moron like you work here?"

Hiding an unhinged smile under my mask, I say, "The desperate kind."

Just as Emily and the nurse come in with a full oxygen tank, the patient yells, "Who's this cunt?! You're not my nurse. You're too sexy for that."

Without a word, the nurse moves the patient's oxygen line from the wall to the tank as the patient throws more insults at her while Emily stands dumbfounded.

I push the wide bed out the narrow door and say to Emily to get her attention, "The people who designed the beds did not communicate with the people making the doorways, giving us less than an inch of extra space to maneuver through."

Squeezing the bed pass the narrow door gap, I push the patient the four hundred yards to dialysis, up the dreaded hill and into the small department. All the while, the patient grumbles curses at the world. At dialysis, I push the patient into the correct bay, then have a nurse sign my paperwork as proof they were dropped off. I warn the signing nurse, "This guy quite a peach."

The nurse says, "I'm well aware."

Outside the department, I finish the paperwork while explaining to Emily what needs to be filled out, but she seems zoned out. I ask, "Are you good?"

She shakes her head to focus. "Yeah. I just…wasn't expecting to be called a cunt and hit on in the same sentence. My last job, I worked for a fast-food chain and my boss was a creep but nowhere near as bad as that."

"Like I said, it's just a job. You can't let it get to you or else this place will break you." I put the paperwork in my pocket. "Be careful because some patients can get handsy too. I once got groped by an old lady."

She lets out a little giggle at that. "How did that happen?"

"When transferring her from a stretcher to a bed." I reenact the move. "I was pulling her over, and she saw an opportunity, took it, and held on tight."

CHAPTER 5
THE ED

THE NEXT JOB IS IN the Emergency Department. "Now the job on the phone never says what's wrong with the patient, but you can assume it's never good," I tell my trainee on the way there.

Emily nods in understanding.

"The only thing you need to worry about in your first week is location. This place is a giant maze, and it takes about two weeks to learn where everything is."

We stop at a four-way intersection.

"For example, do you have any idea where we are or how to get to the Emergency Department, or more importantly, dispatch and the cafeteria?"

Emily looks around at the identical hallways surrounding us. She tries to guess with a troubled look in her eyes. "Maybe back the way we came?"

I point to a sign on one of the walls. "That is one way, it's easier to just follow the signs. It has every important location next to an arrow." Then I point up to the low ceiling, to more signs. "They are a life saver."

At the ED, I take Emily to the most important part of this hospital. "This is the water station." I pour myself a cup of water and open the drawers next to it. "And crackers."

The three drawers are filled to the brim with crackers, one of saltine crackers, one of graham crackers, and one of salad crackers. "Every unit has one of these, but only the ED has salad crackers, the best crackers." I take a few of each and chuck some water. "Stay hydrated and keep the calories burning. I almost passed out my first day on my own because I ran out of calories to burn. The floor shifted as gravity started to win."

Emily takes one of the graham crackers and has a drink of water.

"The other important thing to take from here is pens. This is the only department that restocks pens. Do you have a pen?"

Emily shakes her head no.

"You will need some with all the paperwork we have to fill out for every job. Plus, nurses are notorious for stealing pens. They will borrow one and walk away, never to be seen again." I show her the hidden stockpile of pens before we get the paperwork.

We have to ask around for the nurse because there is no listing for who has which room in this department. The nurse is on hold to give report to the admitting nurse who won't sign the paperwork until report has been given. All we can do is wait, so I take a seat nearby and gesture to an open chair for Emily.

"There's a lot of hurry up and wait around here. Take every opportunity you get to sit down. Your legs and feet will appreciate it."

She sits down, looking unsure about what else to do.

"So, you used to work in fast food. I did a bit of that fresh out of high school. Served ice cream all day. It was busy in the summer but boring as hell in the winter. What did you serve?"

Emily says, "It was a fried fish place. I refuse to ever speak its name ever again. I was seventeen, and my boss kept hitting on me despite being in his thirties. His advances got worse when I turned eighteen."

"So, you came here?"

She says, "Yeah, the hours work great with my cosmetology school."

"Wait, you're in school for hair stuff and you came to a hospital for work?" I stop myself from saying something dumb. "That's quite the contrast."

The nurse calling report says, "The patient has a large metallic object stuck in their rectum."

Our light conversation of getting to know each other stops.

"The patient claims he fell. He's not in much pain, took some Tylenol before arriving. I would recommend against walking even though he walked in here."

We can't hear what they're saying on the other side. I have to fight back the urge to laugh. It's so strange and unexpected, I can't help it.

Once our paperwork is signed, we go to the patient who is blocked by a thin curtain. I look to Emily, "Are you ready for this?"

She lets out a sheepish, "No." Then with a sigh, she says, "But I don't think I have a choice."

I swing the curtain open. "Hello, sir. I'm Sebastian with Transportation. This is my trainee for the day, Emily."

Emily lets out a soft, "Hi," waving her hand from the waist.

"We're going to get you to the Observation Unit and then into a real bed instead of these rough stretchers."

The patient is lying on his stomach, focused on his phone, with a white sheet covering his body, but there is clearly an object pointing out of his posterior region that does not belong. He says, "It's about time. Any idea when they'll be taking this thing out? I really need to fart."

"Unfortunately, I do not know such things. But someone in Observation should know."

Emily keeps staring at the protruding object with her head slightly cocked to the side.

I gently nudge her to stop while explaining how stretchers work. "You can push the stretcher, and I'll show you where to go."

Observation isn't far away. I guide us through the least populated direction, but everyone wants to see. Word spreads fast through this place. I bet even the nurses in Labor & Delivery on the other side of the facility will know before the end of the day.

In the Observation Unit, all the nurses and patient techs stop what they're doing to see this new admit. The nurse is even waiting by the room for the patient. Now that's rare. I usually have to go hunting for them.

I adjust the bed to the same level as the stretcher, explaining everything to Emily so we can work together to move the patient over. Then, while we're putting on gloves, the patient crawls over on their own and leaves the white sheet behind. I get a perfect view of the object. It looks like a silver metal pipe. The nurse quickly cover the patient's shame with a fresh blanket. Once the paperwork is signed, and I toss the stretcher's linen into a linen bin with a biohazard sign. Then Emily and I scrub the stretcher down with bleach wipes.

A sweet patient care technician comes over to us. "Hey, Sebastian. What was it?"

"Not sure, but it was shiny. Maybe a flashlight."

Emily stands there silently looking at us.

"Oh, my bad. Emily, this is Kelly. She used to work in transportation before upgrading to cleaning patients."

Kelly says, "It's more than that. I also get paid significantly more."

Emily greets her with a small hidden smile but is clearly still processing the latest patient.

Kelly asks, "First day?"

Emily nods in reply.

"Don't worry, you'll get used to it. Patients fall on things all the time." She makes quotes with her fingers to imply the lie of "fall."

I say, "You'll develop a very dark sense of humor. The kind that would get you canceled on TV, but it's how we cope. Remember that six-hundred-pound patient we had to move."

Kelly says, "Yeah. For some reason they thought it was a good idea to have the girl with a bad leg help you push that patient."

"I was pushing, you pulled, then halfway through the transfer, you asked if I was even pushing, so I let go to prove a point."

Kelly nods her head while giving me a friendly glare. "I almost dislocated my shoulder."

"We've got to get this stretcher back to the ED. I'll text you later."

Kelly says bye as Emily, and I sanitize our hands before leaving the unit.

Emily asks, "Is there a thing between you two?"

I shrug, "We're just friends."

"But you have her number."

"Yeah, friends have each other's number." It is unwise to go any further. I've seen romances completely destroy workspaces. The stress of the job mixed into a relationship leads to constant fighting and bickering and pulling in innocent bystanders unable to pick a side. That was one of the reasons why I had to quit my job serving ice cream.

Once the stretcher is returned to the Emergency Department hallway, the job is complete, and we get another job also from the ED.

I tell Emily, "This one is only going to get a CAT scan, so it will be an easy job. The patient is under the care of the Charge nurse and is in one of the trauma rooms." I ask the nurses at the nearby desk, "What's the deal with this one?"

They all look to the Charge nurse, who is a veteran of the hospital of about thirty years. She says in her grizzled voice, "Cupid's Bow."

Emily and I look at each other equally confused.

I say, "I'm sorry, but I've never heard that one before."

The Charge nurse signs the paperwork. "You'll see. They're not much of a talker either."

In the room, we find an absolute horror show. Blankets with dark stains thrown around, and in the center is a man twisted into a bow with one hand stuck deep inside his rear end. Both Emily and I stand speechless. This is a new one.

I finally break the silence with my practiced speech. "Hello, I am Sebastian with Transportation, and this is my trainee for the day, Emily. We are going to take you for a CAT scan in Radiology." I whisper to Emily. "Get some gloves and a blanket."

As I step into the room, my shoe makes an unnerving sticky sound. I tell myself not to look, it's best not to know, and shiver slightly as each next step has a residual stick.

Emily returns with a warm blanket to cover the contorted patient. Without a word, he rips the blanket off and throws it at the wall with his free hand. I don't bother saying anything and just prep the stretcher for transport.

The ED the Radiology Department are just a short walk up hill away. We drop off the patient in an open bay and pull the curtain closed for both patient privacy and any passerby's sanity.

The tech working the scanner is zoned out on scanning another patient.

I say, "You have a Cupid's Bow."

While signing the paperwork, they slowly turn to me. "A what?"

"They were self-loving when their hand got stuck where the sun don't shine. They don't like blankets either, so have fun." Then I turn to leave.

Once clear of the department, Emily lets out, "What the actual fuck!"

Washing my hands I say, "Yeah, that was a new one for me too. I've never had two butt blockages in one day. Usually, they're spaced out by at least a few weeks." I finish the paperwork. "Come on, we have a few more jobs before our lunch break."

Emily says, "Sitting down sounds great, but I don't have much of an appetite."

"You will, trust me."

CHAPTER 6
BUGS

WE FINALLY GET A SIMPLE job, taking a Pediatrics patient for an X-ray. The kid is in good spirts and says he broke his arm doing a jump on his dirt bike. His mother laughs and then says, "He broke it falling off a stool that spins."

The kid says, "Come on, Mom. My story was better."

She replies, "Every time you lie, an angel loses their wings."

After we drop them off, Emily asks, "Are you religious?"

We pass one of the few windows. I stop for a moment, basking in the bright light. "I don't really know anymore. This place makes you question things. With faith and God. There is comfort in thinking there is something after this, but at the same time, when you watch a patient slowly decay and then you have to move their heavy corpse to the morgue, you ask how things could be this cruel."

Emily says, "That's a bit much. Were you an edgelord in high school, listening to death metal."

I think back to the music I was into in high school. "Not really. I was into the classics. I also used to play in a band back then, but I haven't seen anyone from the band since I moved out of my parents' house."

Our next job pops up, sending us to take an elderly patient to Vascular. After the nurse signs the paperwork, she says, "They'll need some assistance with transferring," and follows us into the room.

Nothing seems out of the ordinary with the patient until the blanket comes off. His feet are rotting off their legs. As he moves, large chunks of skin remain stuck to the bed sheets. Emily quickly looks away while I slap on my gloves and go in to help move the patient over. Emily calms herself enough to help us, but I can see her making a disgusted face under her mask.

Vascular is a small department across from Nuclear Medicine, on the other side of the hospital. The patient seems surprisingly calm despite their situation, just staring up at the passing lights.

After dropping off the patient, I say, "That wasn't too bad."

Emily says, "That was fucking nasty."

"Yeah, I don't think lotion will do much at that point."

Emily looks at me through squinted eyes.

I say, "Find the humor where you can."

We stop for water, then hunt down the assigned nurse for our next job, another ED admit.

Emily gets to the room first, asking the nurse before she goes in, "Why is there a pile of towels at the foot of the door?"

The tired nurse says, "Bed bugs…good luck."

Then the second I take my eyes off him, he disappears with my pen.

"Where's the protective gear," Emily asks backing away from the door.

"Hospital policy is no contaminated protective clothing in the halls." Trying not to grown by simply stating the facts.

Confused Emily says, "What does that mean?"

"It means we can wear an apron into the room, if you can find one. Then we have to remove it as soon as we leave. Just put on gloves and watch what you touch those little bugs can jump.

Last time I was careless, the bugs followed me home and I had to have my apartment fumigated."

When I open the door Emily does not follow me and I don't blame her. A horrid smell leaks through my mask and fills my sinuses. Emily makes a audible gag as the stench reaches her. The patient is covered in thick layers of dirt and grim. He's out of it, not focusing on anything.

"Hello, I am Sebastian with Transportation, and this is my trainee for the day, Emily. I'm going to take you to your new room."

There is no light of recognition behind his eyes as he points in different directions. As I adjust the stretcher for transport, I can see small bugs crawling all over the man's skin and the sheets. I don't dare touch anything other than the steering handles as I push the stretcher out the door.

Emily keeps her distance for the entire walk. I can't stop looking at the lice moving around this man's long, greasy hair. At the unit, Emily runs off to find the nurse while I set up the room. As I lower the side rails to prepare for the slide over, the patient grabs my arm.

He says, "Don't let them take me."

I immediately tense up, biting down a scream before saying, "It's okay, sir. We're going to get you into this nice, comfortable bed."

"They're after my lucky charms. Don't let them take my charms."

I can see the heroin scars running up his arm. "No one is going to take anything from you. We're here to help you." I want to yell, *Get the fuck off me!* But I know that would only freak him out more. My arm starts to feel ever more itchy. As if his little friends are invading my skin.

When Emily returns with the nurse, he loosens his grip just enough for me to pull my arm away. Leaving behind a dark brown smudge that kind of itches. *Oh no, better not have been infected.*

After we transfer the patient over, I tell Emily, "Get the bleach wipes. We need to sterilize the hell out of this stretcher."

I wash my hands, scrubbing my entire arm with lots of soap until I feel like I've scrubbed off a layer of my skin.

Emily asks, "What do you think was wrong with that guy?"

"Junkie off the street. They're more common than people with stuff stuck in their butts." I finish the paperwork but don't complete the job on the work phone. "Come on. It's almost time for our lunch break." I wait until we are right outside of Transportation dispatch before I close the job so we can take off for lunch.

CHAPTER 7

THE BLUR

L UNCH IS NEVER LONG ENOUGH. Thirty minutes never feels like enough time to eat and rest my feet before the grind calls me back. I give the work phone and Vocera to Emily for the remaining four hours of this eight-hour shift. The job isn't that hard to learn. She just needs the hands-on learning to memorize where everything is, which in turn also means less hard labor for me. We move about fifteen patients in that time, including the peach back from dialysis to his room. He's mellowed out after that session but still hits on Emily, all while looking at me.

Then the second person we pick up from dialysis starts tearing up about halfway back to their room and says, "My chest hurts."

Oh fuck! Is this guy having a heart attack? I immediately go in to panic mode. We were taking the fastest route back to the patient's room. However, this route is far away from the standard flow of hospital personnel, meaning if this patient is Coding, we are on our own to keep him alive.

"Emily! Call the remote heart monitor team. I'll push the patient at double speed."

I take control of the bed while Emily makes the call. I push with all my might, feeling my legs burn. This patient weighs a goddamn ton! *You better not die on me, you bastard.*

I reach the room and call for the nurse. She's busy with another patient.

Emily catches up a few moments later. "They haven't detected any abnormalities."

Then the patient's wife comes in the room and asks, "What's wrong?"

The patient says, "My chest hurts."

Shit, if this guy is about to Code, I need to get her out of here, is all I can think.

The patient's wife says, "Oh, heart burn again."

The patient nods.

You have got to be kidding me. I panicked because of heart burn?! Emily and I exchange knowing glances as if we were probably thinking the same thing.

As soon as my paperwork is signed, I take a water break to catch my breath.

Emily asks, "What would have happened if it were real?"

After a long swig of water and a gasp for air, I say, "Stop, announce Code Blue on our location, and begin CPR. Then get out of the way when the nurses arrive. They have way more experience saving lives. Rich has been here for over thirty years, and he's never had a Code Blue during transport. If a patient is that high of a risk, a nurse will be with you during transport. Or, if the risk is too high, then they won't be moved."

I show Emily how to complete the job and the next job shows up. I tell her this one is "The Histo Bucket."

Emily looks confused once again. At least I think it's confusion. I miss uncovered human expression.

"The Histo Bucket is the post-surgery parts that need to go to the lab in Histology for analysis."

Emily blinks again, not sure how to react.

"I did warn you there would be gross stuff. I just wish someone had warned me about all the old man dick I would see. Moving a corpse is rough, but for some reason, old people nudity is worse."

Emily says, "My grandfather would wander around the nursing home without pants. For some reason, once a man passes a certain age, pants become too much of an inconvenience."

I want to ask more, but we have to jump out of the way of a bed being pushed by four people in dark green scrubs.

Emily asks, "Where are they going in such a hurry?"

"To the ICU to die." My voice is cold, not because I don't care but because I don't want to.

Shocked once again, Emily exclaims, "What?!"

We keep walking to the back entrance of surgery. "In order to keep the number of patient deaths on the surgery table low, they move them to the ICU to die."

Emily tries to say something. "That's...that's..." But she can't find the words.

I say in my dead pan voice, "It's an unfortunate reality of hospitals. That's why most hospitals have the ICU right next to surgery." I have to sigh to buy myself a moment before continuing. "It's not out of malice. It's just an unfortunate fact the hospital has to deal with. Surgeons do their best, but not every surgery is a guarantee. You've seen the conditions most of these patients are in. Everyone is doing their best, but the sad truth is that you can't save everyone."

We reach the back of surgery and ring a doorbell. Out comes a surgeon with a two-foot by two-foot orange box on a gray cart. He takes off his mask and smiles, "Nice and full for you guys. We were busy today. Hold on a second before you leave." He goes back past the red line only surgical staff can cross, then returns with a bright orange bag with a large L-shaped object in it. "Put this one in the fridge when you get to the lab." Then he returns back behind the red line as the door closes.

Emily asks, "Is that what I think it is?"

I say, "Above the knee amputation. Don't get diabetes."

Emily pushes the cart but keeps getting distracted by the severed leg on top of the box.

Histology is a small room in the back of the lab, sharing a wall with the blood bank. I go to put the leg in the fridge, but four other cold severed legs tumble out as I pull the door open. I catch them all, almost gagging because they all have an odd gooey weight to them and smell of decay. I force them all back in with the new leg and close the door before they can tip over. I think Emily is smiling under her mask. Looks like she's starting to grow that dark sense of humor.

I instruct her about how to fill out the ledger, and we empty out The Histo Bucket. There are ten samples from one person. Little white flacks in clear capped cups filled with liquid. Then there's a severed shredded finger in clear cup, a chunk of an ear in another with a gross lump on it, and the final one has an appendix, I think.

CHAPTER 8
MORE BODIES

NEARING THE END WE GET a job for the surgery tower. Post-Op to their room in the seven hundreds. Emily looks uneasy in the large rickety old elevator. To keep the mood light I say, "They need to replace this old thing, I'm fairly certain it was built a hundred years ago."

Emily's eye glare at me not finding any humor in my exaggeration.

"If you want, we can take the stair next time but I'm not carrying a patient down those stairs… again."

I print up the paperwork and the nurse signs it without saying anything. She seems preoccupied with another post-surgery patient. My patient appears to be a heavy-set man with an oxygen tank and a heart monitor. I call the remote monitor office to let them know we are moving the patient and where to, they approve transport. While Emily sets up the bed.

After Emily pushing the patient to the elevator I lean against the wall. Enjoying having someone else do the heavy lifting for a change. Two more hours to go, almost out of here. Then the elevator stops but the door don't open.

Damnit

Emily looks at me expecting me to know how to fix the old elevator.

"It's all good should be moving again in a moment." I say into my Voicera, "Call Dispatch."

It rings and rings but no answer. So I say again just a bit louder, "Call Transportation dispatch!" Only to be met with more ringing. I take out my personal phone to see I have no signal.

Well ain't that just great!

"Guess we're stuck here for a bit." I say out loud to Emily and the unresponsive patient. Nothing else I can do so go back to leaning against the wall and wait. Until the patient's heart monitor begins to appear sporadic. "No need to worry the doors will open soon." I say trying to keep everyone calm. As the patient enters cardiac arrest.

Shit!

I press the emergency button on the elevator wall. As the patient flat lines.

Crap, Crap, Crap! What the hell do I do?

I yell into my Voicera, "Code Blue!" as I climb onto the patient and begin chest compressions. Feeling her ribs crack as I press down trying to stay on the correct rhythm. All the while my Voicera continues to ring. Emily freaks out and begins to bang on the metal doors and yell for help.

Sweat drips down my face as I continue chest compressions. I forgot what my count I'm one not bothering to give a recue breath as the patient has an oxygen tank flowing continues air. "Somebody answer!"

When the elevator doors finally open my patient died long ago. I fall off the bed as a Nurse takes my position of chest compressions. Sweating profusely and unable to catch my breath I remain on the floor. While an emergency crew takes my patient away.

Before my heart rate mellows out. I receive a call to return to dispatch. "Emily, can you help me up?"

She takes my hand, pulling me back to my feet. She is absolutely lost for words. So I say, "That was not our fault."

Still in shake Emily stares past me.

I grab her by her shoulders to shake her back to earth. "Emily! That was not our fault. That patient should not have been transported. The nurse did not warn us that patient was a high risk. Nore did the remote monitors. We had no way of knowing. And the failure of the elevators was beyond our control."

She almost says something in disagreement, but I speak louder. "The weight of that loss does not belong to either of us. We did everything we could."

At dispatch I give a full report of the incident with Emily. There is still an hour left of the shift. We are given the option to leave now or work the last hour. I accept the last hour, needing the money. Surprisingly Emily want to finish the shift as well.

CHAPTER 9
HOME

WITH ONE LAST TRANSPORT BEFORE the shift ends, Emily and I take the patient in a wheelchair from surgery to the front lobby. Emily takes the stairs this time while I use the smaller public elevator typically use for people before surgery not after. She has just had shoulder surgery and doesn't require a night in the hospital to recover. I would guess she is in her late thirties. She's pouting nonstop and I don't care enough to ask why, it's too close to the end of the shift to care. We have to wait for a bit until her ride brings the car around. She finally speaks insisting, "I can walk I don't need help from the likes of you."

I just say, "It's hospital policy, even if you are fine. If you suffered any kind of injury on your way out, we would be liable."

When the women's mother arrives, Emily opens the passenger door, and I offer my hand for support. She spits out, "Don't touch me incel!" Slapping my hand away as he awkwardly gets into the car.

As the car drives away, I ask, "What the hell is an incel?"

"Involuntarily celibate." Emily says without skipping a beat.

Crap...

Suddenly I feel very lonely. I'm twenty-six, and I've never had real a girlfriend. I tried in high school, but I was rejected each time. Then in college everyone already had a significant other. Did I miss my chance to pair off?

I press that feeling down along with all the others. My shift is over, and I need to go home and eat some real food. That will help me feel better.

Emily goes to the boss to talk about her first day, leaving me to wonder if I'll see her tomorrow. She's probably traumatized from watching someone die. While I honestly don't feel much. I did all I could in the moment. In the end it's just another body for the fridge.

I turn in all my paperwork, making sure everything has the same date, then stapling it all together and dropping it in the box with everyone else's papers to be documented into the computer. As the next shift starts coming in, each of them with a coffee cup in hand, I say my goodbyes to the dispatch team and the others ending their shift. I take the long walk back to my car at the top of the parking garage. It's uncomfortably hot from sitting in the sun all day. Even though summer hasn't officially started, here in the Arizona you can feel it just around the corner. I nearly burn myself when I touch the metal seatbelt buckle. With a roar from the old engine my fourth-hand rust bucket slowly comes back to life. My drive home is short since I only live a few miles away. I don't have money to stop for food, there should still be some canned goods in my reserves.

My studio apartment is on the second floor, facing east. The first step is broken and has been since I moved in three years ago. My home is lacking most furniture, but I have a bed and a table with one chair. The singular room contains my kitchen as well. I check the sink to see if the water is back on. Nothing comes out, they've been working on the pipes for three days now. With a sigh, I grab a cold-water bottle from my fridge, and zap it in the microwave for a few seconds before entering my bathroom through the closet. Technically, the closet is only a small corner with some cloths and a dusty guitar case actually in the bathroom, all one room. I have to be careful not to waste my precious water, so I decide to shampoo my hair tomorrow.

After stripping off my sweaty scrubs I take a shower using my lukewarm water bottle with a few holes stabbed through the cap and some hand soap. It may be cheap, but I feel better. I have another shift tomorrow, so I stretch to keep the soreness at bay. I haven't gained much weight since I started this job. I am glad this job keeps me fit, but all my muscles shifted from my upper body to my legs. My pants feel tighter around my thighs and calves than when I was exercising in college.

My dinner is some crackers I stole from work and minestrone soup eaten from the can as I don't have the water to do dishes. I read a newspaper I also swiped from the hospital, while I add up my finances. I'm going to need to pick up some more shifts if I want to go back to school. I'll need to work more than forty hours a week at my current pay rate, but that will make classes harder to deal with. Can't afford another student loan.

My phone buzzes with a text from Kelly. "Hey, how was your shift?"

I reply, "Not bad. My trainee did most of the heavy lifting. What about yours?" Rather not talk about my dead patient.

"Very interesting. That guy you brought in livened up the shift. Turns out he had a flashlight stuck up his rectum. I also got into an argument with my supervisor again."

"I bet he said he fell on it."

"He did!" she types in all caps.

"That's what they all say. What was your supervisor angry about?"

"I didn't fill out some paperwork correctly. It's whatever though. She's never liked me."

I need to think for a minute, then I reply, "Why don't you transfer to another unit?"

She doesn't respond for almost an hour. "No, I really like working in the Observation Unit."

As I sit alone in my apartment with the only sound being my fridge humming behind me, I decide to take a shot. "Do you want to do something this weekend? There's a new arcade in town that serves beer."

Another hour passes.

My thoughts spiral. *Crap, did I overstep? I shouldn't have said anything. I'm such a goddamn idiot.*

Then she says, "I'm free Saturday."

Yes! I text back, "Great, I'll see you then."

I feel proud of myself for about ten seconds, until I remember my schedule. I work Saturday, and I can't cancel the shift. I need the money too desperately, especially if I'm about to pay for a date. Maybe I can switch shifts with someone.

CHAPTER 10
ANOTHER DAY

THE NEXT MORNING, I STRETCH before my shift, mumbling about how I'm going to ask my boss for a shift change. Then I put on the same scrubs from yesterday, not having any cleaner options. I'll need to do laundry after work, assuming I can get enough quarters. Once again, I park at the top of the parking garage.

When I clock in, my boss informs me of another morgue run.

I can't keep my mouth shut. "Really Rod? Does night-shift refuse to move corpses?"

Not seeing the humor, he says, "They do, but the morgue is full. So, I need your help to take the body to the morgue and another one back to their room. I've been switching them every hour to keep them from rotting before the funeral home people arrive."

I feel a gross unease in my spine at that, but I push it all down along with my dried spaghetti breakfast. This is the job I signed up for.

Rod is kind enough to help me with this run. He says, "I wouldn't make a subordinate do something I wouldn't."

"I really appreciate that. When I worked in food, my bosses would never let themselves get dirty."

As we remove the body from the room, I figure I might as well ask now. "I need to take tomorrow off. Can I switch shifts with someone to make it up?"

Rod says, "Actually, I need someone for the nightshift tonight, if you think you're up for it?"

"I've never worked a nightshift before."

"It's similar to day shift but less happening. Most of the testing facilities are closed. Just specimen runs and emergency department admits."

"I'll take it," I reply, thinking I'll just need to catch a nap before I see Kelly.

As we move a cold corpse onto the metal stretcher, Rod says, "Good, I'll change your schedule after this."

Back in the office, I see Emily leaving with Rich. He gives me a high five as we pass, and I say to Emily, "Glad to see you back."

She says, "I almost didn't."

Rich says, "It all gets easier." As they walk down the hall, I hear Rich ask her about her musical interests.

The day continues like all the others, in a blur of faces covered with masks. As I strain my body to push patients from one place to another, Nurses are stressed and take it out on me. I do see one doctor in the distance, I think, but it could just be someone in a white jacket.

Near the end of my shift I enter the 950s Unit for a routine CAT scan transfer. Should be an easy way to end my shift, will probably be able to get over an hour rest before my night shift starts. Only to find a patient in a wheelchair yelling at a nurse. "Get the fuck out of my face bitch!" with what looks to be a small white pencil in her hand.

While the nurse ties to calm her down. The patient places the pencil in her mouth and pulls out a lighter.

The nurse's calm leaves as she yell, "There is no smoking in here!"

Someone else yells security. While several nurses appear out of the blue all of them attempting to restrain the wheelchair bound patient. The patient scream at the top of her lungs just before biting someone's arm. A security guard rushes past me throwing his full weight into the crowd of people sending the mass to the ground. The lighter slides out to me. I stop it with my foot noticing I'm right next to the oxygen tank storage.

Knowing another body in the mix would only cause more chaos. I walk past giving the lighter to the front desk receptionist watching the wrestling match with the wheelchair patient. "That wouldn't happen to be my patient in 960 bed 1, would it? The notes do say combative."

The receptionist says, "Oh, no he's a separate issue."

"Terrific." I say with far too much sarcasm. As the wrestling match ends with the patient being forced back to their room.

Once I get my paperwork signed, I enter room 960 saying my overly practiced line. "Hello, I'm Sebastian with transportation. I'll be taking you for a CAT scan."

The patient doesn't say anything just stairs at me blankly. I notice his arms and legs are in restraints, probably can't transfer to a stretcher safely. After preparing his bed I grab a mask hanging from his I.V. pole. "You'll have to wear this in the hallways." But when I go to put it on, he lunges at me his teeth jagged bared. Biting the mask out of my hands just missing my finger by a fraction of a millimeter, yet still close enough to feel his limps enclose upon me. In a delayed reaction I jump back freezing. Then as dignified as I could, I leave to find the nurse. Who is currently with the patient across the hall. "I don't think the patient in room 960 is safe to travel." Interrupting her as she talks to her other patient.

She turns around glaring at me. "Don't interrupt me!" Her voice cold.

Maintaining professionalism I say, "I'm sorry, but that patient just tried to bite off my finger. There is no way they won't do worse when they are transferred to get scanned."

"He's fine, with partial paralysis he can't do much. And I don't have time to leave the unit. Now get out of my face!" Then she proceeds to ignore me.

Nothing more I can do here. So I take the patient. As soon as I enter the main hall a senior nurse demands to know why my patient doesn't have a mask. I pick up the torn mask sitting in the bed, handing it to her "You try." The patient snarls at her. She quickly leaves us both alone.

At the top of the hill in the Radiology department I deliver the patient to CAT scan.

The technician says, "Perfect timing. Help us load him onto the machine you can do a round trip."

I was hoping I could just drop of this mess of a patient and clock out for the day but of course for once CAT scan doesn't have a line. "Sure heads up he's a violence risk, a biter and apparently partially paralyzed."

The technician say, "Understood. Barry get the straps."

Barry a much larger technician nods and sets up the scanning table with wide scraps that will completely wrap around the patient, while I inform Dispatch to make my job a round trip. When the table is ready the three of us prepare to move the patient unhooking from his bed. He immediately begins to flail his arms around smacking Barry while biting at me, once again barely missing. His legs don't move but with much resistance as a team we pull him over and strap him to the scanning table. After a two minute scan, the fight starts again. This time I get slapped across the cheek. Leaving a solen red lump. While Barry gets bitten in the arm. But in the end I get him back to his unit. The same senior nurse glares at me in the hallway but I don't make eye contact, I've got bigger fish to fry. The nurse signs the paperwork without a word. In the end I completed the job ten minutes after my shift had ended.

In Transportation Dispatch I clock out. There is no point wasting the gas to go home. Instead I rest my head in the break room until it starts all over again.

CHAPTER 11

NIGHTSHIFT

I DON'T REALLY SLEEP, JUST REST my eyes, before my phone alarm wakes me for my nightshift. After a good stretch to the skies, my back pops. "Let's do this thing."

My first job is an ED admit to room 405. I suppose it could be worse. The patient is an old man in his nineties and keeps asking me for my name. I tell him, and he tells me his name is Ralph, then he asks for my name again and the cycle repeats. At his new unit, several nurses and patient techs follow me into the patient's room. They even grab the patient slide board for difficult patient transfers, making me wonder if they know something I don't.

Once in the room, the nurse says bluntly, "Welcome back, Ralph. Now we're going to move you to your bed for the night." He then turns to everyone else, "You guys ready?"

Ralph exclaims, "I'm not going anywhere until that screen has my wife's phone number displayed." He points at the TV on the wall currently playing the food network.

The nurse focuses on the task at hand. "Tilt him for the board."

We turn him on his side to push the slide board under him.

Ralph then grabs the stretcher's railing and refuses to move. The patient tech has to peel his fingers off while the rest of us pull him over to the bed. When he lets go, he simultaneously smacks me in the face and craps the bed. They hadn't put down any absorbing pads before we got here, but that's not my problem anymore. I readjust my mask over my damaged face, get my paperwork signed, and take my stretcher away to sanitize it.

The next several jobs are patient admits, all of them heavy. Either that or fatigue is starting to set in. The time reads almost midnight. I find a place to sit down in the dark, empty hallway as my legs burn from strain. I rest my phone on my shoulder, so I can hear my next job notification. My eyes feel heavy, as if they carry the weight of the world.

BING!

I shoot up from the dead. How long was I out? My phone reads that six minutes have passed. I don't think anyone saw me dozing.

Patient needs blood in the ED. That's going to be a long walk. I have to go all the way to the ED to pick up paper-work, then got to the blood bank, then head back as quick as possible to not let the blood go bad.

The ED is absolutely packed with patients spilling into the hallways. One screams in pain, ripping out their IV line while a nurse tries to calm them down as they are sprinkled with blood. The nursing station is full of nurses trying to call reports to admit patients. I take the paperwork and get out of the way as fast as possible.

I really don't like the lighting in Buck Hall. I know it's dark out, but it's the same brightness as it was this morning. It's unnatural. Then I notice someone knocking on the door to the morgue. That's odd because no one goes in there except transporters for drop off and they wouldn't knock. Could be the funeral home people, but they're really late today.

I call out, "Hey, buddy, you got to talk to the lab people first."

There is no answer. I walk closer, thinking they must have ear buds in or something.

When I reach where the person was standing, the hallway is empty. *Where did they go?* I swear I hear a whisper "Sebby." as a cold chill runs down my spine. Instinct kicks in, making me blurt out, "Nope!" and then run to the lab at full speed, not stopping until I reach the blood bank.

At the blood bank, I find a lone person listening to something really loud on their headphones while enjoying a red lollipop. He's the first person I've seen not wearing a mask today. His mustache hair sticks to his sugary treat. His lack of awareness gives me a chance to catch my breath.

When he finally notices me, he leaves the pop in his mouth and signs the paperwork, then retrieves a packet of blood from the fridge without leaving his rolling chair.

Back in the hallway, I look both ways to see if I am alone and then power walk at high speed to safety. The whole time I tell myself, "It's fine. It's fine. No need to panic. It's a hospital. People die here every day. Of course it's haunted. It's normal, perfectly normal. Everyone here has seen a ghost at some point, I'm sure. That was just my first."

I look back down the accursed hallway and see what looks like an old man in a hospital gown with short white hair, and dark shadowed eyes standing just outside the morgue. Then in a blink he's gone. My walk turns into a run until I reach the ED.

The nurse thanks me for the speedy delivery, then goes to her unconscious patient with what looks like broken legs.

I don't get another job right away, so I find a place to sit down next to an older nurse drinking a large cup of coffee as she does computer work. It feels safer in this chaos than in the silent hallways now.

When she notices me, she says, "You alright? You look pale."

"I'm good. I think…I think I saw a ghost."

Unfazed, she asks, "First nightshift?"

I nod in reply.

"Avoid going to the Pediatric Unit. Now, if you don't mind, we are understaffed, all the admitting rooms are full, and there's a full moon tonight."

This place is full of death. Lost souls wander the halls alone. The end is inevitable and more likely than not, I'll meet my end in a hospital, hooked up to a machine, waiting for the darkness. I pray that I'll have someone by me when that time comes.

CHAPTER 12
FIRST DATE

I GET TO SHOWER WITH WARM water for the first time this week, a few hours before the sun rises. Then I turn off my humming fridge and set my alarm for an hour prior to my date, before passing out.

I dream of being locked in the morgue fridge, my body freezing as I fumble with the door and scream to be let out. "Help! Please, I'm not dead! I'm not dead!" The door opens and I fall to the ground, crawling through the small room, my voice hoarse from screaming. I am alone in the darkness. A pale old man looks down at me. "You are a disappointment."

My alarm blares, but I still feel tired. The clock reads noon-thirty. My body feels sore. I forgot to stretch before bed. I pop my back, then prep for my date and rush out the door.

Oh boy, I actually have a date! I won't be alone any longer. *Okay now, calm down,* I tell myself. *It's a first date, don't expect anything to happen. This is just getting to know each other better.* I finally got my paycheck and all my bills were paid with the last check, so I can live a little. Probably should get some quarters for laundry while I'm out.

Kelly is waiting outside her apartment in a sundress with jeans underneath. She looks wonderful with her bright hair down. I've only ever seen her in scrubs with her hair in a tight bun. I button up the top button on my collared shirt, which is the nicest thing I currently own. I get out to open the car door for her.

She hugs me. "It's good to see you."

"I'm happy to see you too." I can't remember the last time I got hugged, that wasn't a patient attacking me.

At the arcade, we order a beer and place an order for food to be ready in an hour. The arcade has two stories of gaming machines. The first floor is full of Japanese rhythm games and mini games to win tickets and racing games, while the basement floor has claw machines for prizes as well as shooting games. Kelly wants to start with the racing games. We pass by a professional rhythm game player as they put on grip gloves before selecting the hardest level.

I buy us a token card for forty dollars, equal to four hundred tokens. We play the games on the first floor while trading stories from the hospital.

Kelly jokes about one encounter, "That's when she throws her bed pan at me, yelling, 'To Valhalla!' I slammed the door to her room shut as the liquid inside splashed against the glass. Needless to say, we did not move her that day."

I laugh before asking, "Why Valhalla?"

She says, "Warriors can only enter Valhalla by dying in combat. I guess she thought she was on the way out."

We go down to the basement floor. I have a particular skill I developed many years ago that will make her very happy, for I am a master at the claw machine. I analyze the many claw machines, looking for the perfect prize, something Kelly will want and that will be easy for the claw to grab. Soon I find an animal from an Anime show she'd mentioned watching, then secure the prize in three attempts.

She asks, "How did you do that?"

"I spent all of my allowance as a kid on the claw machines at the supermarkets. While my parents would be shopping. Then I would give the prizes as Christmas gifts to my siblings and cousins."

"That's so sweet." She hugs the plushy, then me.

"You're very welcome. I think our food is ready."

The food is mediocre considering the price, but Kelly seems to be enjoying it. That's all that matters today.

After several hours of playing arcade games, I take her home. I don't make a move because this is only the first date, but I say, "This was fun. Let's do it again."

She agrees, but says, "Let's go for a hike next week, and maybe a picnic."

"I know just the place."

CHAPTER 13

BACK TO WORK

I RETURN TO WORK MONDAY WITH a renewed outlook and clean clothes. The soul crushing reality of this place can't hurt me today, for I finally no longer feel alone in this world. We may not be boyfriend and girlfriend yet, but we are surely on the way. *Oh, Kelly I can't wait to see you again. Hopefully, I'll get a patient in Observation and get to see you early.*

Most of the day passes like all the others, moving bodies from one place to another. After lunch I get a patient to go from Observation to Pre-Op, and I hurry over faster than I should. Once I get to the Observation Unit, Kelly is nowhere to be found. I thought she worked Mondays, but maybe she's just on lunch break.

I ask the receptionist if she's seen Kelly.

She replies, "I'm not allowed to say."

Now all my joy leaves me as I am filled with worry. *What happened? Is she hurt?* I text her, "Are you alright?"

Then as soon as I drop off the patient to the second third floor Pre-Op, Kelly calls me crying, "They fired me."

Well, that's bad. "Oh, I'm sorry—"

She keeps talking right over me. "Because I wasn't filling out the paperwork right. But my patients were fine. We've been understaffed for so long that I had to slack on it to tend to all my patients. I don't know how they can afford to fire me. My supervisor is such a bitch! I don't know what I'm going to do! I'm too low on money to pay for both rent and food this month. I can't afford both without a paycheck."

While she takes a breath I say, "It's going to be okay. I can help you with groceries this week."

She calms down a bit. "Really? You would do that for me?"

"Yes, I know what it means to go hungry. All my bills were paid with my last check. I have some money to help out, and with my new overtime, I'll be fine."

"Thank you, Sebastian. This just came out of nowhere and since my sister lost her job, I've been the only one with income."

I keep my voice calm. "It's going to be okay. I'll call after my shift, and we can go grocery shopping." Hanging up as I enter the elevator.

Shit, this paycheck is going to evaporate before I know it, but at least it's for a good reason. Yet I feel oddly claustrophobic. I press the ground floor of the elevator again. I've stopped moving. "Oh, Come on! Really?" The elevator has stopped between the second floor and the first. I press the button again but nothing happens. Rich did tell me the second floor was haunted by a ghost. Letting out a frustrated "Damn it." I kick the elevator door and the machine comes back to life, completing the few feet to the ground. I'm going to take the stairs next time.

My final job is a morgue run for the patient in room 405. He must have passed while I was on my date. At least the fridge is empty today, so no body Tetris. I refuse to die alone like Ralph did. I'll do whatever it takes to have someone special in my life to the end. I refuse to be an incel anymore.

Kelly is waiting patiently outside her apartment for me as I drive up, while I'm still in my scrubs. She happily kisses me on the cheek. "Thank you for doing this."

At the store, she gets a shopping cart and starts dropping items in as we walk down the aisles. I've lived alone on a minimalistic budget for so long that I barely fill up a hand basket when I go shopping. This is probably going to drain my accounts. I have to remind myself that I did offer to help, and now I guess that means both her *and* her sister.

I end up spending over two hundred dollars on food. The first time I've ever broken three digits at a grocery store. That's way past my planned budget, but it's too late to back out now. I'll have to live off ramen, canned soup and stolen crackers for a bit longer. I remind myself that I am doing a good thing and suffering is okay if it's to help another suffer less.

I take her back to her apartment and help put everything away. Then she gives me a big hug, thanking me before sending me away.

I sit in my car for a full minute and then ask my reflection in the rearview mirror, "Did I just get used?"

CHAPTER 14
AUTOMATION

A S I MOVE ANOTHER PATIENT across the hospital, they grumble about how I should be replaced by a machine.

"You know at least once a week someone mentions that to me. However, it's not so simple. I have put a lot of thought into this. First of all, you would have to replace every single bed in the hospital. Each normal patient bed costs about two thousand dollars, not including pillows that are always in short supply, and there's almost a thousand rooms in this place. The ICU has the most advanced beds. They have motors, but they can't pull the bed on their own still requiring someone to push. We also have a special bed called a High-Low bed that is specifically designed to lower all the way to the ground. They are also the hardest to steer. So, I can only imagine that buying roughly a thousand beds with motors will cost more than just paying me a buck more than minimum wage to move you. Also, the issue of plugging in the beds to charge may seem like a small thing, but someone would have to do it. Or there would have to be tracks to every possible location, which would require the entire infrastructure of the hospital to be redone. And as of right now, it takes them about twelve months to retile twenty feet of this nine-square-mile hospital. Not to mention the fact that the chapel has been under construction for over a year apparently."

The patient seems to have stopped paying attention, but I keep going to fill the travel time.

"Then the other issue arises with automating my job in particular. There are too many human elements that would offset the computer's timing. Nurses need to put in reports in an exact way, but they are always rushing and under-staffed. Treatments and testing material would have to be gathered on an exact time frame. That simply is impossible if any part is human operated. So, a hospital would have to be built from the ground up to be automated and everything controlled by a central computer. With a computer having access to all possible knowledge in the world makes it sound like there would be few mistakes, but I can guarantee there would still be mistakes because patients lie and are not obedient drones. Replacing human care for a robotic one will result in mechanical mishaps. People should be in charge of taking care of people even if it's not perfect."

I push the patient up the dreaded hill.

"That being said, some mechanical aid would be appreciated on these tougher sections."

Another transporter sees I'm struggling up the hill and comes to my aid. When we reach the top, I say, "Thanks, Pete."

He gives a thumbs up and keeps on his way.

"Above all is the power issue. The cost of powering everything would be extremely expensive. It would also be extremely dangerous if the electricity was ever cut, with either very few people around to help or none. The patients would suffer. Also I've yet to see a computer be able to predict a junkie's next move. I once watched a man rip out his small intestine thinking there was treasure up his butt. If a grizzled nurse of thirty years comes up short in that situation, no computer can even compete."

CHAPTER 15
PICNIC

Day five of 12 hour shifts. My mind and body are deteriorating but I'll have a nice fat paycheck at the end of this. My feet ache more than ever. My only relief is short rests I can get in between jobs during yet another night shift. Sitting in the one of the many wooden benches lining the main hall. I lean back resting with my eyes open for sleep is far away.

All I can hear is a child crying just beyond the corner at the end of the hallway, even though I am far from the pediatric unit. The sound echoes unnaturally in the dark empty halls. There is a fear bubbling in my gut. Yet it is overpowered by my lack of energy as all I want to do is sit here until I get another transport job.

The crying child begins to hit the wall with an almost even rhythm. Yet I remain seated refusing to care, until I my phone rings with a job. Forcing myself to my feet I walk down the hall toward the sound as it distorts into an unnatural pitch. When I turn to corner there is nothing there. As the sound stops. I pause to take a long blink then continue my journey, hearing an uneven knock coming from the other end of the hallway.

I'm not sure if there are actual ghosts or if they're just illusions in my exhaustion. I have a constant feeling of always being watched even when I know I'm alone. Shadowed eyes are near. I think I'm reaching the level of numbness everyone else on night shift is at. I don't want to treat death and the unknown with callous disregard because it's just another day at work. Yet each shift, I give less and less attention to the windows of death, just to give a few moments of rest to my sore feet in between transportation jobs.

The one bit of light in my life is tomorrow my only day off this week. I'll be taking Kelly on a little hike to a nice picnic with a great view of the city. I made some sandwiches and got a small vegetable platter that was on sale.

When the day of our date finally comes. Feel as though I should spend the day sleeping moving as little as possible. No! I will not throw away my one chance to be with someone special. After a quick stretch, a shot of pure caffeine and an ice cold shower I leave to pick up a beautiful women to spend the day with in nature.

Kelly waits for me outside her apartment but when I open the car door she gives me a letter before getting in.

I ask, "Should I read this now or later?"

"You can read it now," she says as she sits in the passenger seat.

I open it up and give it a read while walking around back to the driver's seat. In it, she confesses how much she likes me and how appreciative she was for my help.

"Does this mean we're dating now?"

She blushes a bit. "Yes."

"Does that mean we can kiss?"

She nods her head, beckoning me to her. Our lips meet in a brief moment of passion before she pulls away. "Let's go for this hike," she says.

At the trail head, I notice she's walking kind of slowly. "Is your leg injury acting up?"

She says, "I should be fine." Playfully pushes me forward. "Now it's your turn to tell me why you became a transporter? You've mentioned you went to college."

I take the lead, knowing this hike well. My parents liked to take me and my siblings out here all the time when we were young. "Criminal Justice was my goal. I wanted to be a police officer like my grandfather. He would tell me stories of his time on the beat before he passed. I was committed to getting my degree before the academy. Anyone can apply to the police academy but with a degree I would move through the ranks much faster. In the end it didn't matter I got permanently denied for being colorblind. I had no idea I was colorblind. I found out at the end of the recruitment process, during the doctor's physical."

"Wow, what colors can't you see?"

"Dim shades. Dark blue looks purple to me. Or brown and red tend to bleed into each other unless it's a bright red but that can bleed into orange very easily. As a result, they said my testimony could be thrown out of court. As a result the police academy told me to go away and never come back. So, I now have a degree I legally can't really use unless I go back to school, which I can't afford due to my current student loan debt. Thankfully, I had gotten a CPR certification on the way. That's how I ended up in hospital work. After a brief year of cleaning pools but I digress."

"Really? That's so unfair."

"Think about it though. I could put out an All-Points Bulletin on the wrong person. Someone in a blue shirt commits a crime and some innocent person in a purple shirt gets arrested instead. What about you, why did you choose the hospital?"

"I want to be a paramedic." She doesn't say why. Instead, she tells me all about where she grew up in northern Arizona over the next thirty minutes it takes to reach our destination.

We sit on some big rocks in the shade as we eat and then hang out for a long time just talking. Kelly does most of the talking. I just listen to the story of her life. She goes through her childhood, her parents' separation, and her sister's alcohol recovery, laying all her trauma in front of me. Eventually, she's ready to go home, but her leg cramps and she struggles to walk. So, I offer to carry her back to the car. She hops on to my back, and I begin the march. This should be easy. I move people three times her weight every day. Why is this even remotely hard? Then I hear her start to cry.

I say, "It's alright. I've got you."

She buries her face into my shoulder. "It's not that. You're just so nice." She then confesses the dark truth of how much of a monster her father was.

The abuse her and her sister suffered from him leaves me feeling sick. I'm not equipped to deal with this. I'm no therapist. Yet, I have to do something. "He's gone now. You never have to see that fucker ever again. You should be proud of how far you've come without him."

Her crying slows, and she thanks me.

She doesn't kiss me when I drop her off, just says, "I'll see you soon."

I spend the drive back to my apartment just trying to process everything she dropped onto me.

CHAPTER 16
YET ANOTHER DAY

I'M TIRED, HUNGRY, AND DON'T care about your problems right now. However, I can't say that to the patient as they tell me their life story while I push their massive load up hill to Radiology.

"That's when I met my third wife. That sweet thing knew how to work a shaft, if you know what I mean."

Panting at the top of the hill, I let out an exhausted, "Sure."

"Oh, are you one of those virgins? How old are you? You should have cashed in that card years ago. I guess that's to be expected. Women like a real man." He slaps his gut with an echoing sound. "You outta try to hook up with one of these sexy nurses around here. You can tell they're thirsty," he says as a nurse passes us before whistles at her. She acts though she did not notice, or maybe she just doesn't care. My patient clearly didn't see the wedding ring on her hand.

Most of the nurses are married with such thoughts left outside the hospital. This isn't a place to feel horny, only tired or depressed.

He starts talking about his exploits in Taiwan, "There are streets in Bangkok where the women are so desperate for a real man they will walk up and grope you. Cheapest best nights a man could ask for."

When we finally reach our destination I cut him off, saying, "I wish you the best with you ultrasound today, sir." Then I quickly rush off to get my paperwork signed.

The techs are in their office, chatting about hospital gossip. I clear my throat to get their attention. They don't stop talking while signing my paperwork and sending me away.

As I pass the patient, he tries to say more, but as I keep walking, I just say, "They'll be right with you, sir."

Safe in the hallway, I close the job. Then my phone buzzes but not my work phone. My personal phone received a text.

Emily passes by, asking with a bit of tease in her voice, "Who you talking to?"

I say, "Kelly. We've been texting me all day. I've been too busy with patients to respond most of the time."

"So, you did ask her out. I thought you were afraid of workplace romance."

"I am, but she doesn't work here anymore." I ask, "What's your next job?"

"Seven hundreds to X-ray."

"Mind if I walk with you? I've got a patient in the six hundreds."

Emily nods with a smile that reaches her eyes, and we set off.

I ask, "How are you liking the job so far?"

Emily pulls her mask down to show a bruise on her cheek. "I punched by a homeless man during my first job today."

"Ouch. Did you hit him back?"

She says, "No, but I was tempted to. I did nothing to provoke him but just lost it when I entered the room with the nurse. How do you deal with people like that?"

"You have to get good at your dodge." I demonstrate my well-honed skill by pulling down my mask to show the fading welt from being smacked six days ago.

Emily asks, "What is wrong with this place?"

"How should I know? I do the same job as you. We got dying drug addicts coming in off the streets and sick people on their way out. All we gotta do is move them from one part of the hospital to the other."

When we reach her destination I wish her luck.

"Thanks, Lord knows I need it."

When I reach the 600s I finally respond to Kelly. She starts conversations, but then only gives me one-word answers, meaning I have to completely carry the conversation. However, when we are together, she is extremely talkative. There could be worse things. She suggests that we get food and watch a movie tonight, which honestly sounds great. I could use a simple night for once.

After a normal eight hour shift, I stop by my apartment to clean up, then drive to Kelly's apartment. Both her and her sister hop into my car. Kelly kisses me on the cheek but pulls away before I can kiss her back. They want to go to a fast-food joint nearby, which also works for me because my wallet is getting thin. Taxes took away so much of my overtime, then the bills came to clean out the rest. I used the last bit to get ahead of my student loans but I'm nowhere near paying them off. How does it cost so much to live in a studio apartment? They get in line in front of me. I never said I was paying, but I guess I am. It's fast food though. How expensive could it be? Then I walk up to order a five-dollar chicken sandwich and learn the total for all three of us comes to sixty five dollars. My blood turns cold as I begin to sweat on the inside of my body. How the hell did they order over fifty dollars' worth of food from here? I have to use my credit card as I don't have enough in my wallet or in my checking account currently.

We return to their place with two heavy bags full of food and my singular chicken sandwich. They put on a romantic comedy from the '90s. I laugh but fight to stay awake after I finish my food. Sadly, eventually gravity wins and I close my eyes. Kelly kicks me out as soon as the movie ends.

CHAPTER 17
QUIET

ANOTHER DAY OF WORK AHEAD, my first job has me waiting to be able to take the patient. The paperwork is all signed, but the nurse needs to take the patient's blood and give her meds before I can take her. So I patiently wait, deciding to text Kelly and ask what she has planned for the day.

She replied, "Nothing much."

"Then maybe we can spend some time together."

Her reply is a simply, "Ok."

We are going to have to talk about this situation in person. I text back, "I'll think of something."

She doesn't respond to that one, leaving me to wait as I listen to the sounds of the hospital. The beeping of an IV machine from a nearby room. Incoherent screaming from a patient down the hall. Mumbled gossip from the nurses.

A patient walking the hall says, "Wow, it sure is quiet."

The nurses stop talking and glare fire at the shuffling patient. There is no such thing as quiet around here, and saying otherwise out loud will inevitably jinx the calm.

The fire alarm blares and an even louder voice comes over the loudspeakers. "Code Red in Unit 800. I repeat, Code Red in Unit 800."

That's this unit! I look around, catching a glimpse of smoke from the nurse's break room, as all the doors automatically close to contain the fire. There's a small amount of smoke coming from the microwave. Someone must have put aluminum foil in there again. Nothing I can do about it, so I take my patient to her destination, having to open every closed door in the main hallway.

I wonder what would happen if there was a serious fire. It's not like it could spread very far without accelerants. This place is made out of inflammable materials, drywall and concrete. Even if there was serious damage, the hospital wouldn't close. There would probably just be another section under permanent construction like the chapel by the cafeteria.

By the time work ends, I still haven't come up with a plan for Kelly tonight. Things were just too busy. It doesn't matter though, she bails on me. She says she has a family situation, not wanting me to get involved. So, I just go home to my studio apartment, where I stretch and eat before heading off to the shower in my bathroom/closet, I take a moment to look at my dusty guitar case. It's been years, and I wonder if I even know how to play anymore. Thinking probably not, I leave it where it is and take my shower.

CHAPTER 18
LAST DATE

KELLY INVITES ME TO DINNER at her place with her sister. Excited, I go. Also, my food supply has been very bare bones lately. I've been paying for almost all of her expenses, including last month's rent. Now that I think about it, she hasn't let me kiss her since the picnic. She gave me that love letter, but she won't let me get close. I do respect her space, but this doesn't seem to be the issue. She will kiss me on the cheek, but she won't let me return my affection. She only allows me to shower her with my limited finances.

Is this how a relationship is supposed to work?

It's also a bit early for dinner. It's not even four in the afternoon. Maybe we'll finally have a talk about this relationship. I have so little experience in the love department. It's time to clearly define what this is.

When I knock on the door, she opens it to reveal dozens of moving boxes.

"Sebastian, thanks for coming. I have a bag for you."

I'm caught off guard by the sight of everything. "What's going on here?"

"We're moving upstate to live with our mom. We can't really afford this place anymore." She hands me a bag of some of the groceries I had previously bought for her. "Also, can you take this box to Goodwill for me?" She pushes a heavy box of junk into my arms.

"Wait, when are you moving?"

Her sister yells from the bathroom, "Tomorrow morning!"

I look back to Kelly. "So, what does that mean for us? I thought we were a thing."

She says with a smile, "I guess you'll have to wait. I'll probably be back in a year or two." Then she closes the door, leaving me alone in the apartment hallway.

I let out a weak, "Goodbye," as I hear Kelly tell her sister how nice I was. Then I hear both of them burst out laughing.

At Goodwill, the guy taking the donations asks, "Moving?"

"No, but my girlfriend is."

He smiles. "And she's going without you. I know that pain." He goes to slap my hand in respect.

I expect him to bump my knuckles after, but instead he grabs my hand and pulls me in for a bro hug. I pat his back once before we separate.

He says, "My ex did the same thing to me dude."

I say, "Maybe being alone is easier."

He corrects me. "No, but it's cheaper."

At home, I examine the contents of the bag Kelly gave me. An open bag of spaghetti, a half-used jar of marinara sauce, a potato, and a full bag of flour.

Might as well use the stuff that's been opened. Best not to let food go to waste. Sitting down to eat my solitary meal, I run through my head everything that transpired between Kelly and I and finally reach a simple deduction.

"I was too desperate, but a least I got spaghetti."

CHAPTER 19

A FRIEND

THERE IS NO TIME TO feel sorry for myself as I have to work. This has been my first shift all month without a morgue run. Instead, the day is filled with talkative patients all wanting to tell me their life stories. At first it is interesting and a reason to stay out of my own head. However, toward the end of my shift, I start to tune them out.

I get a job for an ED admit, age seventy, name Walter Richards. The name sounds familiar, but I can't place it. He's most likely a frequent flier.

The Emergency Department is relatively calm today. There are very few people in the hallways, but it's still hard to find the nurse in charge of my patient. Eventually, I get them to sign my paperwork and I take the patient. He looks really familiar, but I can't place him. Maybe if he takes off his mandatory mask.

The patient is kind of out of it, cognitive but just a bit loopy. I wonder what he's in for. They never tell me what issue the patient has. It's rare to get so much as a violence risk warning.

In the room, the patient stares at me a moment and then says, "Sebastian, is that you?"

I answer with a bit of hesitation, still not recognizing him. "Yes…?"

He takes off his mask. "It's been too long my man. Are you still plinking that guitar?"

In that moment, it all comes back to me. My next-door neighbor, growing up. When I was thirteen, I played in his folk band. He gave me a guitar and taught me how to play it. I was the youngest by forty years, but that didn't matter because it was fun. I looked forward to coming home from school because I wanted to jam out with them. Until I left for a band my own age in high school. That feels like a lifetime ago.

I take off my mask. "Jesus…Walt. I…It's good to see you."

He says, "Wish it was under better circumstances."

"Yeah, me too."

He takes out his phone. "Check out this new guitar I bought." He shows me a shiny yellow Fender telecaster.

"That's real nice. You still jamming with Mark and John?"

He rolls over to the bed from the stretcher. "Nah. John died a few years back, and Mark got cancer. But you're still jamming, right? You had joined your friend's band didn't you? You had a real talent for playing."

"I've been busy. New job and all." Truth is, I haven't touched the guitar in a long time, but I can't tell him that.

The nurse comes in and signs my paperwork, then tries to shoo me out.

As I am pushed out, Walt says, "Keep in touch."

I say, "I'll be back later to check on you."

After cleaning the stretcher and returning it, I stand in the hallway for a moment, reliving the many great jam sessions we had. That was a time when I felt invincible, when

I could conquer the world with only six strings. Now I feel lost. Do I even have a purpose anymore?

The rest of the day is busy and doesn't give me a chance to get back to Walt. An hour before my shift ends, I get a text from an old friend from high school wanting to get a drink. I reply in agreement. I could use a drink.

Nicolas has been my friend since freshmen year of high school. He introduced me to Ben and started the band that would go on to win the high school talent show. I do the math in my head, realizing I hadn't seen Nicolas in over two years. I've let time get away from me.

I meet Nicolas and some of his university friends at a bar a few miles from the hospital. There wasn't time to go home before the scheduled gathering, so I show up in my scrubs. On the bright side, this pair was washed recently.

As I walk into the bar, I see Nicolas laughing with his friends. I approach their table, and he immediately stops what he's saying to greet me and give me a hug. "Glad you could make it, buddy."

I forgot he was a hugger. This is the first human contact I've had since Kelly dumped me last week. Even when I was with her there wasn't much physical contact.

I order a beer while Nicolas gathers everyone's attention. "My friends, thank you all for coming. I have a big announcement. I'm getting married."

Everyone cheers for him. I give him my congratulations, then change my order to just gin and tell the bartender to keep my tab open. I had no idea he had a girlfriend, after his brutal breakup with Lilith years ago. They kept trying to pull me into the arguments, thinking about it I haven't seen Lilith in even longer. After they broke up I stuck with Nicolas as I had a longer history with him. He declares another man to be his best man, even though I've known him far longer than anyone here. Yet, I completely understand why. I've been absent from my best friend's life for a long time, and the best man introduced Nicolas to his current fiancé. The hospital has consumed me.

The night still goes well. We all drink and talk. Nicolas catches me up on his life and his current engineering work. It's mostly top secret advanced technology stuff, but he seems to have a real passion for what he does.

Then one of his coworkers comments on my attire. "Are you a doctor? Tell us what's it like treating people."

I smile at that. "I'm not a doctor."

Worried that he offended me, he says, "I'm sorry. Are you just a nurse?"

With a chuckle, I say, "No, I'm a last responder."

The group looks both horrified and confused by that comment, so I continue, "I move bodies in the hospital. Both alive and dead. As well as objects and parts. People die every day, and we can't leave them in the bed because there's always someone new needing the attention."

One of the engineer friends says, "That's just dreadful. Someone should make a machine to do that kind of dirty work."

Another one of these guys. "That wouldn't work. For one, the power usage would not be cost effective versus paying some dude a buck more than minimum wage to do the same job. As well, moving live patients wouldn't work because patients can be…how should I say this? A bit exotic. No, that's not the right term. Let's just say, *unpredictably crazy*. There ain't a super computer on this planet that can predict a crackhead's next move, that take instinct. That's why you will rarely ever meet a nurse in a good mood. They are on the front lines with the chaos."

Nicolas seems to get what I'm saying, but the others look a bit confused.

I continue, "Just today I got the wrath of a patient who refused to get an CAT scan because they claimed to no longer have heart disease. This dude was four hundred pounds and could not walk. Then there was another patient who the nurse said could walk just fine before ditching me, but when I entered the room, the patient was missing a leg from a very recent amputation. The staples were still in the stump."

The night continues as I drink nothing but gin until I am way to messed up to drive home. Nicolas and most of his friends get a lift home from a designated driver, leaving me alone at the bar. As I finish my seventh drink, I notice I'm not quite alone in this place. There are a couple of fairly attractive women at the other end of the bar.

Filled with liquid courage, I approach them. "Hello, can I buy you beautiful ladies a drink?"

They look me up and down, two of them walking away laughing. The third says, "Ew, I have a boyfriend," before leaving to join her friends in the bathroom.

Once again, I am alone. So, I pay my tab and leave. I don't bother with my car, needing a walk to clear my head. The night is cool, with few cars on the road. Everything is quiet for what feels like the first time. What the hell happened to me? I'm disconnected from my best friend and live in absolute solitude. I wish I could have more, but no one wants me for anything other than money. Which is something I don't have very much of. Is it time to accept that I will die broke and alone?

As I walk past a bus stop, a twitchy man in dirty, ragged cloths steps in front of me. He doesn't look me in the eye as he stands at a contorted angle. "Spare some change for the bus?"

My wallet is literally empty. "No, man. I'm broke too."

He pulls out a rusty blade. "Give me something, man."

Oh shit. I put my hands out. "Whoa."

I notice his skin is rotting and he has nothing but crooked bits of teeth in his mouth. This guy is a junky, probably on fentanyl. I slowly step back. "I ain't got shit, man."

He makes an aggressive step forward. "Don't play me. I know you got something!"

My wallet is empty except for my driver's license and an almost maxed credit card, and I don't want to go through the hassle to replace those. My phone is in my back pocket, and I don't want to lose all my contacts. Is this junk worth my life? Is my life worth anything right now?

The crack head moves closer.

"I have nothing."

He moves within striking distance and yells, "Give it to me!" waving his knife just in front of me.

Without a thought, my right leg swings upward and lands hard in between the man's legs. He falls down whimpering in pain. I turn and run as fast as I can, like a scared rabbit. There is no destination, just fear pushing me forward for what seems to be forever until my lungs force me to stop. I cough as I try to catch my breath. Then I throw up the entire contents of my stomach onto the sidewalk.

When my body stops trying to kill me, I try to gauge my location. As I realize that I ran right back to the hospital, one thing goes through my mind.

Walt.

CHAPTER 20
THE LAST RESPONDER

I STILL HAVE MY ID BADGE in my pocket. Lucky it didn't fly out while I was running. Sobriety has creeped back now that the contents of the night's drinking coat the sidewalk. With my ID badge on, I enter the hospital. Visiting hours are over, but no one is going to question a man in scrubs in the hospital. After a quick stop for water, I make my way to Walt's room.

The attending nurse doesn't give a damn why I'm here as long as I don't cause any problems. Walt is still awake, just watching TV. He's hooked up to oxygen and an IV and a bunch of things to monitor his vitals.

When I enter, he mutes the TV and says, "Glad you came back."

I say, "Of course. Sorry I'm late."

"Don't sweat it. Just glad you're still kicking."

"As best I can."

He gestures to the seat by his bed. "Tell me, Sebby. What have you been up too?"

"Surviving as best I can. Always feels like there's too much and yet never enough. I thought I had it all figured out. Now I have no idea what I'm doing."

With a smile Walt says, "That's life, kid. It's slow every day until, boom! You're an old man. Enjoy every moment, even the bad, because it's over before you know it."

I don't know what to say to that.

He grabs his phone from the nearby table. "I still have some recordings of our jam sessions." It takes him a moment, but he eventually finds it.

The sound is crude, but I can hear everyone. Walt on lead guitar, John on drums, Mark on violin, and me doing my best to strum the rhythm. It takes me back to that day, when all that mattered was enjoying the music. I miss those days before the rejection in college, the disqualification at the Academy, the dangers of cleaning pools, and the soul crushing of the hospital. We listen to those recordings for hours, until Walt falls asleep and I pass out in the chair next to him.

I wake up in the morning to the sound of the alarm on my phone. My head throbs with a hangover. "Shit, I've got to work today!" Then I remember where I am. At least I don't have to rush.

I don't wake up Walt. He probably needs rest, considering his predicament. I use the nurses bathroom to give myself a bird bath, then ask the attending nurse if she has any ibuprofen for a headache.

She says, "Sure do." And takes out a large jar of pills and pours out a handful as if she was giving me candy.

"I don't take these very often."

"Oh. Then one of these should do it." She then stashes the bottle back in her desk.

I hunt down some crackers and patient jello before I start my shift. Right when I clock in, a Code Blue is announced for Walt's unit. I immediately feel a pit in my gut as I rush over.

"Please no!"

The Code Blue is canceled, but I keep going and reach his room as nurses are exiting.

"No…"

I find the attending nurse as she goes to fill out paperwork. She recognizes me from last night and says, "Heart attack. There's nothing more we can do."

I stand there paralyzed wanting to cry but no tears fall.

She puts her hand on my shoulder. "It's not your fault. At least he had a friend for his last night." Then she leaves to fill out the paperwork for the diseased.

My shift drags by slowly while I dread what is to come. When my work phone buzzes with a morgue run, I am tasked with taking Walt's body to the fridge. I don't want to refuse this job. There is a need for me to be the one to do this. I remain stoic for the entire job as I place him onto the cold metal cart. My coworker, Pete, doesn't say much during the job, but he rarely talks anyway.

"Goodbye, my friend." Then I close the large metal door of the morgue shut before taking the paperwork to Pathology.

The day continues like all the others. Moving people and parts where they need to go. After work I have to walk back to the bar to pick up my car. There's no sign of the crack head. Maybe the sun is keeping him at bay.

At home I stretch, shower, and eat a can of soup. Then I take out my dusty guitar case and open it for the first time in forever. My old acoustic Epiphone stares back at me. It probably needs new strings and a neck adjustment. After a tune, I strum a chord. It hurts my fingers with a sharp metal pain, my calluses have long faded, but I strum another chord, then another, until the old songs come back to me. I mumble the words off-key, but it doesn't matter. I keep playing the same four chords over and over until another song comes to mind and I play that. Letting my voice grow louder as I project with confidence, I play until my hands ache and my voice is hoarse.

I never want to forget the music again.

CHAPTER 21
CRISIS RESPONSE CENTER

DURING A NAP ON MY lunch break my phone rings with an unknown number. The area code is local. Might be a family member with a new phone. It could also be a former pool customer, should tell them I ain't their pool man no more.

"Sebastian?" a woman's voice asks.

I say, "Maybe, depends who's asking."

"It's Lilith. Remember from the band." Her voice sounds desperate.

"Oh, yeah. What's up?" I haven't spoken to her since her and Nicolas's break up. Wanted to keep my distance. The whole thing was unpleasant to put mildly. Wonder if she knows he's engaged, I'm not going to bring it up.

"I need your help..." She pauses for a moment.

Why do I feel déjà vu right now?

"Can you pick me up."

That's not so bad. I can give a ride, pulse it would be good to reconnect. I didn't leave in the best way. I ask, "I can when I get off work. Where are you?"

She says sheepishly. "I'm at the Crisis Response Center."

I've heard of patients in the Emergency Department ending up there when they are a threat to themselves or others. "What are you doing there?"

Her voice now filling with rage. "My stupid ex got me sent here. The fucker crashed my car then called the cops on me. I mean what kind of a narcissist does that. He should be the one in here not me! Now they won't let me leave unless someone can take me and I don't know who else to turn to."

"I can pick you up after my shift today." I'm still rebuilding my finances after Kelly.

"Thank you! Thank you! Thank you! You're the best!" She exclaims through the phone.

Four hours later of pushing bodies my shift ends. I drive to the Crisis Response Center which turns out to be still on the hospital's property. I work in the main hospital but there are dozens of buildings sharing this chunk of land. There are private practices for doctors and even a hotel for people visiting sick family. The Crisis Response building is in the back of the property far away from the main roads. It looks exactly like the all the other hospital buildings. A gray building with fake wood to match the adobe desert theme with a poorly lit sign displaying the title.

Inside I meet the an over worked receptionist reading emails. I clear my throat to get her attention. She glances at me, "I don't have any messages regarding patient transfers."

I realize I'm still in my scrubs. "Oh no, I'm off the clock. I'm here to pick up a friend in need."

The receptionist keeps her eyes on her computer but I can see the screen change based on the reflection on her glasses. "Name?"

I say, "Sabastian Scott here to pick up Lilithnifer Bean."

"You must be a very good friend to help out that one." She says clicking through profiles

Concerned I say, "What's that supposed to mean?"

"I cannot disclose patient records but I will say she is a frequent flyer around here."

Terrific, what the hell did I just sign up for now. I could still bail, no I promised I'd pick her up.

"Just sign here." She hands me a clipboard with one sheet of paper on it.

"Is that it? No forcing her to take meds or even a background check on me?"

The receptionist says, "No, she doesn't have any criminal charges this time. I just need proof someone picked her up."

After signing the paperwork I take a seat in the empty lobby. Remembering the last time I saw Lilith. Her, Nicolas and I all worked at the same ice cream shop. The busy days in the summer time we would work as a well-oiled machine knocking out order in lighting speed. Then in the winter months when the crowd slowed down, I would only work with one of them and talk all through our shift to pass the time. Nicolas and I would talk about music and how we wanted to take the show on the road. Lilith and I would do the same but we would just talk about life sometimes. We could talk about anything for hours. Then after we would close up shop for the night we would all meet at Ben's house to jam out. It was simpler back then before we had to rent the jam space downtown.

When Lilith and Nicolas broke up they would fight none stop. It got so bad that they couldn't work together but neither of them wanted to quite their job. I had to work double to keep them apart and they would only complain about the other during our shifts. When I quite for the Police Academy I thought I was finally free from the drama. Only to end up cleaning pools in the Arizona Summer.

Finally Lilith walks out. She's a bit of a mess with her air all frizzed out and her cloths a bit ragged. She lights up when she sees me with a smile stretching from ear to ear. "Sebastian!" She runs up almost jumping on me with a massive hug.

Unsure of what to do I pat her on the head. "It's good to see you too."

She holds on until I give a gentle hug back. I'm not so good with these things. Case in point everything that just happened with Kelly.

Lilith takes me by the hand, "Let's get out of here."

In my car I ask, "Where to now?"

"Your place." She says as if it were obvious.

"Not your place? Are you still at your parent's?"

She says, "I just need a place to crash for a bit."

"I see… than I should warn you. I don't exactly live in luxury." As we drive to my studio apartment.

There is no fear of silence for just simply asking, "So how are things?"

Lilith tells me all about her life. "God's been fucking with me real hard lately. Been charged with everything lately. All bullshit claims been keeping me down."

I say jokingly, "At least not murder." Trying to cut the clear tension in the car.

"I almost did."

That was not the answer I was hoping for. This may have been a mistake.

She leans her head on me. "But that's all changed now that you're here."

Then again I'm sure things will work out.

Back at my apartment complex. I try to tamer Lilith's expectations, "It's not much but it's home. And watch your step the first step is broken." Catching her before he goes up the stair case.

Before I open the door I notice my heart is pounding, am I really this ashamed of how poor I am? "There really is much." I open the door to my studio apartment complete with a small bed and table. "Thirsty? I have bottled water." I can't tell if the look on her face is disgust or pure shock.

Oh no, I grossed her out.

She says nothing as her mouth attaches to mine shoving her tung down my throat. As her arms wrap around me. The shock almost knocks me off my feet, instead I stumble back closing the door. We separate for a moment as she strips off her close. I hesitate in awe of her beauty before doing the same. She moves with experience as I try to keep up with her. She ends up on her back beckoning me in.

"Wait, just a second." I grab a condom I had originally bought for Kelly.

Instinct take over for the first time in my life as an awkward passion builds between the two of us. She begin to a moan with desire as I my breathing intensifies giving every ounce of myself to her until a great release.

I collapse to the floor next to Lilith both breathing heavily. That felt quick but I am absolutely spent. Lost for words she wraps her arms around me cuddling into me as she rests her head on my chest. There is nothing but heavy breathing as we lay together. I have no idea what to do next. I can't believe I just had sex for the first time in my life. That all happened so quickly, arguably a little too quickly but in my defense that was my first time.

My stomach aces as I have now worked a full day of pushing bodies eating crackers. Now had an additional workout.

"Are you hungry?" Knowing that Lilith won't want canned soup and ramen.

Lilith perks up from my chest. "I'm starving!"

"What was the name of that place we would go after gig? They had the best tacos." Also the cheapest in the city.

"El Nico's taco stand! I haven't had those in forever. Let's get some!" Her excitement seeming genuine.

It makes me happy to see her happy. I place a delivery order on my phone while we continue to lay there. "It's going to be about forty minutes."

Lilith says, "That's plenty of time." As she pull me to my shower in my bathroom closet. Pausing for a moment when she sees my guitar case. "Are you still playing?"

"I just picked it up again last week."

She says, "I haven't touched my keyboard in a while but I hear Ben has hopped on with a new group. I think their name is Metal Hunters or something like that."

Thank god the water is working today. As we spend the next thirty minutes in the shower cleaning each other. I mimic what I have seen online from my many years alone. While Lilith does things that I have never seen before.

When the food arrives, we dry off with my only two towels. Sitting on the floor we eat tacos. This may just be the best night of my life so far. "Lilith, I had no idea you felt this way about me."

While eating a taco she manages to say, "Of course, I love you."

That causes me to choke on my taco. Once I get my breath back under control. I am at a complete loss for words. After everything I just went through with Kelly and the loss of Walt. To hear someone say they love me means so much. My eyes feel watery, I wipe them dry while Lilith is distracted with her taco. I want to live in this moment forever.

CHAPTER 22
FIGHT FOR YOUR LIFE

AFTER THE GREATEST NIGHT OF my life I have to return to work the following morning. I still need to rebuild my finances. Lilith says she's going to hang out at my apartment, she needs to get somethings straightened out privately anyway. Not wanting to pray I leave her the Wi-Fi password and head back to the hospital.

The day is an adventure same as all the rest. A nurse yells at me for interrupting her while she's giving report, but my mind is elsewhere. I wish I could take this day off to spend it with Lilith. After an unneeded amount of frustration the nurse signs the paperwork for me to take the patient to get an x-ray. The rest of the day is a blur of pushing beds. The only notable thing is another person with a flashlight they "*fell on*." Even that was barely notable. I have truly become numb to this place.

To be fair I keep getting distracted by texts from Lilith. She keeps wanting to ask me about what I'm doing. I don't have time to explain through text, plus I believe that would be illegal, so I simply say "working". Until about lunch time when I actually have free time to respond she goes silent. She probably had to deal with something important.

While stealing crackers in the Emergency Department the Charge Nurse finds me. "Sebastian?"

I stand there with a half-eaten gram cracker in my mouth, "Wha up?"

She has a look of absolute indifference, "Your brother is in the lobby."

I don't have a brother, maybe it's Nicolas. Probably hurt himself and is hoping I can get him a bed faster. Swallowing down the large unchewed chunks of cracker I ask, "Really?"

"He asked for you by name. I saw you were in the area figured I'd just get you to avoid using the intercom. Said he's having stomach issues. Just talk to him while we find an empty stretcher."

Perfect timing that I was in the area. I don't know what Nicolas is expecting me to do. Yet I go out anyway. In the E.D. Lobby I don't see anyone familiar. Just a bunch of people sitting away from each other. Then my eyes meet the much taller man standing next to the doors that separate the lobby for the E.D.

His face flashes red upon the sight of me. I try to say, "Can I help you." But I'm cut short as a fist impacts my face knocking my to the floor.

"Fuck you! You little bitch!" Are the words I believe to be yelled at me as I struggle to comprehend my new perspective. I'm lifted by my scrubs than thrashed about. As more incomparable insults are spat at me. Before the lobby security guard pulls him away.

He yells, "You messed with the wrong guy, Sebastian!" as he kicks the Lobby security guard in the nuts before running away.

The Charge nurse helps me sit up. "I'm so sorry, I didn't know you had issues with your brother."

I rub at my swelling jaw. "I have no idea who that person was."

Her face goes pale, "I can't believe I just sent you out to get assaulted." She shakes her head, "Ok, this is what happened you went out to help a patient get up when that guy assaulted you. Understood."

I can't be mad at her, this is my fault for just going out here. "Yeah, I got you."

She's trying to avoid liability, completely understandable. There are so many regulations in the hospital corporate structure that it interferes with basic patient care. Bending the rules and lying about it later is standard practice. Besides we frontline workers have to stick together.

With an ice bag for my swelling jaw I have to fill out an incident report. That is given to police for the attack. Security footage is collected as well. One of the cops seems familiar. I have to ask, "How do I know you?"

He says, "We took criminology together. You also beat me in the two mile physical to get into the academy."

"Oh, yeah. James right."

"Yeah." Then he asks the one question I didn't want him to ask. "What are you doing here?"

"I got permanently denied for being color blind. And no I didn't know I was color blind until they tested me." Preemptively answering his next question.

James says, "Bummer." Brushing away my clear disappointment. "Well we'll look into this guy. See if we can get a positive I.D."

Then he leaves with his silent partner. While I wonder what my life could have been. I should have lied on the colorblind test. How hard would it have been to memorize the right answers? Not hard at all. Then I would be a cop without integrity. A life without integrity ain't worth it to me.

I end up working the rest of my shift on light duty. So no beds or bodies which is a nice change of pace. Just specimens for testing and blood bank runs, all light stuff but a lot of more jobs before my shift ends.

When I get home, I don't find Lilith anywhere. She left the door unlock and she's not answering my calls. I hope she's alright. Can't do anything about that so I begin my post work stretching routine. Only to be interrupted by someone banging on my door. Nervous I check the peep hole before opening. Thankfully it's just Lilith.

I open the door, "Is everything alright?"

She barges in, "No! My boyfriend is going crazy. As if the fucking psycho has never made a mistake before!" She starts rummaging through my cabinets. "The jackass cheats on me then has me sent to the crisis response center than cheats on me again than has the balls to call me a liar. He's the fucking liar!"

I feel like I'm missing context. "Your boyfriend? You said ex-boyfriend last night"

She makes an exaggerated sign as if I should have known that. "Yes, Fucking Julio. Calls me up than just starts yelling at me for no reason. I tell him about you then he starts making fucking threats."

"Is Julio a real tall guy?" I think I see where this is going.

She glares at me for interrupting again. "Yes! He rejects my apology even though it's his fault for cheating in the first place." She starts waving her hands around. "Then he starts saying I'm going to kill that fucking geek. He trashed my room, broke my T.V." She kicks my table over. "My T.V! That I bought with my money!" Her voice cracking as she keeps getting louder. "My money." Then just screams at the top of her lungs until her lungs are empty.

In the only moment she quiets to take a breath I say, "Calm down, it's going to be ok."

She turns her anger to me, and I realize I said the wrong thing.

"How the fuck would you know that. This is your fucking fault!"

I try to say, "How?"

But she cuts me off. "You abandoned me. It was because you left me behind." She pushes me as tears flow from her eyes, "You left me!" She pushes me again. "How could you leave me so easily!" She pushes me again. "I loved you!"

Her pushes tuner to hard slaps. I catch her arms, "What are you talking about? I left the band to pursue my life's ambition to become a cop." She tries to pull away, but I hold tight. "You showed zero interest in me throughout the entire time we were in that band. As I recall you were dating Nicolas remember."

Lilith kicks me in between my legs dropping me to my knees. As I hold my manhood in an attempt not to puke.

"Nicolas cheated on me with a fucking slut! That he's now marrying! The creep."

Shaking I return to my feet. "No, he's not. He met someone at his engineering job."

She screams, "Shut up!" Grabbing something sharp from one of my draws. "Shut the fuck up! You don't fucking know anything!" Marching at me filled with rage.

I put a handout expecting another slap. "Woah, calm down."

Then I feel a sharp pain in my shoulder. Everything becomes silent I look over at the handle of a knife sticking out of just under my collarbone.

I drop back to my knees holding the exposed end of the knife. Lilith freezes unable to speak as she stares at the damage, she just caused. She almost reaches out to me but stops just to mumble, "I'm sorry…" before running out the door.

I feel warm liquid ooze down my body staining my scrubs before pooling onto my carpet floor. If I pull out the blade I could bleed to death. I've seen it happen at the hospital. The mere effort of breathing hurst as the action moves my lungs to just touch the blade. When I try to shift my body upward a burning pain shoots through my body. What can I do other than sit here and bleed.

Just beyond the door stands a pale figure with short white air and dark eyes. "I'll be seeing you soon Sebby."

CHAPTER 23
EMERGENCY WAITING

I DON'T WANT TO DIE HERE. The knife pierced me just below my collarbone but above my lungs. No one is coming to check on me as my body slowly drops blood. I can't scream as my body is unable to inhale enough air. I have to make an awkward shuffle to my phone on the kitchen counter to dial 911. As my left are hurts to much to move.

Leaving blood smears on my phone I make the call. "This is 911, if this is not an emergency please hang up and call our nonemergency number." Then I am placed on hold as every second ticks by the pain increases. After five minutes that feels closer to an eternity a dispatchers answers. "This is 911 what's your emergency?" says a happy voice.

"Umm help, I have been stabbed." Feeling awkward about how cheery this person is.

"I'm sorry to hear that. Are you safe?"

"I'm in my apartment. The blade is still in my chest."

"Well, don't pull it out. I will send police and emergency services to your location."

Why does it sound like this person is smiling at my pain. I give her my location then there is silence for a while until I ask, "Do I need to stay on the line."

"You are under no obligation sir." As the music holding music plays again.

I hang up. Not wanting to hear cheer right now. So I just sit there in silence with a white dish towel slowly turning red waiting for help. "I've lost control of my life."

After another eternity I hear footsteps coming up the stairs. James calls out, "Police Department."

I shout back, "In here."

James comes in with his partner. "Hey, Sebatian! Long time no see. What have you got yourself into now? I just got report of a domestic disturbance. A woman was shouting in here than ran away."

"Yeah, she went nuts than stabbed me." I point to the knife in my chest.

"I'm going to need the woman's name."

"Lilithnifer Bean."

James shares a knowing look with his partner.

"What was that?" Demanding to know what they know.

James says, "She's kind of a frequent flyer around here. We had to take her to the crisis response center the other day for being a danger to herself and others."

"Based on her in coherent screaming. I'm going to throw out a guess that her boyfriend and her have a toxic relationship." I'm hurt physically but there in another pain I'm trying to ignore that she didn't actually love me. I was just the unlucky soul she used to hurt her real boyfriend. "How far away is the ambulance?"

James says, "We're here for the domestic disturbance not an emergency injury." He looks around at the squalor I live in. "You do know an ambulance ride is over two grand, right?"

The will to live leaves me. "I can't afford that…" Plus the price to get stitched up I can't afford any of that. Maybe I can fix this myself. I grab the blade ready to pull it out.

James grabs my hand before I can do anything stupid. "I'll get you to the hospital."

The hardest part is getting down the steps as each step shakes the blade. With the help of James and his silent partner we get to his police cruiser long before the ambulance arrives. The back seat is hard plastic clearly designed for an easy wash. My wound is going to need to be thoroughly cleaned before it can be closed.

"James…"

Focusing on the road he grunts to know he can hear me, "Ya,"

"Do you like being a cop?"

"It ain't easy. I've seen some fuck up shit doing this. Had to preform CPR on a kid at a car accident then deal with a crackhead head stealing toilet paper from a McDonald the same day."

"I once had a crackhead get his own hand stuck up his butt. Code Cupid's Bow"

"Fucking crackheads."

We share a chuckle at that. It really hurts to laugh

James walks me into the ED Lobby. Where there is going to be quite a wait. An all-points bulletin rings on Jame's radio of shots fired at a nearby grocery store.

I grab him before he goes. "Did that kid survive? The one you had to do CPR on."

Jame's face eyes see something a million miles away. "No." Then he runs off to do his job leaving me to wait for medical attention.

The clock ticks by as blood still drips onto the floor at my feet. As the Lobby is packed with people. All with their own issues. There is a kid with a broken arm screaming at the top of his lungs. A man puking dark liquid into a trash can. The smell of fecal matter assaults out sinuses as another man shits his pants. I'm probably going to die here aren't I.

A pale man with buzzed white hair and dark eyes. Sits across from me. His face uncaring at my suffering. He does not wait for his turn for treatment. No, he waits for me.

How much blood have I lost now. Looking at the increasing size of the blood pool at my feet. Not sure but enough to ruin one of my few pairs of socks. I'm still scheduled to work tomorrow.

"Shit…"

"Sebatian." The pale figure says but the voice doesn't match it's too feminine. "Sebatian!"

It's the nurse calling my name. Finally it's my turn. Lightheaded I try to stand slipping on the blood pool. "Jesus Christ! How long have you been bleeding?"

"Aaaaaa…" Trying to do the math in my head but only seeing haze. "A few hours, I think."

I am helped on to a stretcher as the lobby receptionist is yelled at not for letting me nearly bleed to death but for a possible biohazard. I am taken to a room where I am left alone again while I hope they are getting a blood order. After another long wait a nurse comes in to check me.

"Hey, Sebatian what brings you I in for a visit?"

I don't recognize this nurse, but she knows me. Words are hard right now so I just point to the protruding knife in my shoulder.

"Oh! We'll get a CT scan to see what has been punctured then get you sown up."

My response is a simple thumbs up with my good arm.

They can't give me blood until after the CT scan. A transporter takes me my vision clears up just enough to see. A beautiful young woman with long blond hair. "Emily? I thought you quit." I wish she didn't have to see me in this condition.

Emily says, "Leave of absence, I had a family situation. Had to switch to nights for a bit." Her eyes clearly locked on the knife. "What happened to you?"

"Isn't it obvious. I fell trying to do a handstand in the kitchen." Trying to smile away the pain.

I think she smiles at that, but I can't tell through her mask.

I have to wait another hour to find out the blade missed the important stuff. Unfortunately the anesthesiologist can't come in so they're going to remove the blade with me awake. They cut off my shirt to see the blade clearly. I'm given some anastatic to numb the pain and told to look away. It still hurts when the blade is finally pulled out, but I can't help but to stare. The numb feeling of something being pulled from my body feels unnatural. Followed by blood bubbling out. The pale figure stands over me he places his boney frail hand on my head as my eyes blur into darkness.

I awake alone in a clean hospital gown my bloody scrubs in a grocery plastic bag. Thankfully they left me my pants. My wound now bandaged I look around for a means to tell the time. The blood IV in my arm keeps me from leaving the stretcher even though it has run dry. Sitting up causes a new soreness unlike when the knife was still in me. I find my blood smeared phone with my ruined clothes. It is three thirty in the morning; I work in less than four hours.

Need to find scrubs fresh scrubs for my shift. The gift shop sells scrubs, a bit pricy but I ain't got any other options. My car is back at my apartment complex. Maybe I can call out. I check my phone again. The screen stays black, terrific it just died.

No press the call nurse button by my stretcher but one checks on me for an hour. Right when I am ready to pull this needle from my arm a nurse finally appears.

"Sebatian good to see you're awake. I have your discharge papers. Do you have anyone to pick you up?"

"No, I have to work today."

"I would strongly recommend against working for a while." Horrified by my comment.

"How else am I going to pay for this? I know blood ain't cheap." After filling out all the paperwork. I ask, "When I get billed for this can I get an itemized receipt?"

"I see you know the secret to not get over charged."

This is still going to suck up most of my paychecks for a while.

Wearing a hospital gown as a shirt and all my possessions in a blood-stained grocery bag. I hobble painfully to dispatch just in time for my shift. My ID badge has dried blood on it but still works on the door pads. Upon opening the door I say good morning to my coworkers.

My Manager, Mrs. Fall asks, "What happened to you?"

"I got stabbed yesterday. Spent the night in the ED." Trying to make it sound like it's no big deal.

The shock is clear on everyone's faces even with their masks on.

Mrs. Fall says, "You are not working today. Come with me to the office."

I follow her expecting a lecture. Instead she says, "Are you ok."

I shrug than wince at how much that hurt. "Sort of... not."

She says, "I'm putting you on a two week medical leave of absence. You are in no condition to work."

"Yeah, that's probably a good idea but I can't afford to not work for a month."

"Sebatian, you have never used any of your time off. You have plenty of sick time. I'm also giving you an additional medical leave due to injury." She shows me my accumulated hours on her computer. "You will be fine. Heal up this place isn't going anywhere."

I go to all the transporters waiting in the break room for their shifts to end. I ask, "Can I catch a ride home with someone? I don't live very far, about less than ten minutes."

They all look at on another no one wanting to volunteer. Rich says, "Sorry, I rode my bike here."

Everyone else shares in awkward glances with one another. No one wanting to volunteer except for Emily, "I can."

"Aren't you starting your shift?" I don't want to sound ungrateful, but I don't want to her to lose her job.

"You really did lose a lot of blood." She smile her gorgeous smile. "I worked the night shift remember."

It's refreshing to see her face uncovered. Then again, I could be delirious from blood loss. I need to be careful not to say anything stupid out loud.

Walking to Emily's car she comments, "Nice shoes." Giggling a bit at my attire.

My feet are covered in bright neon yellow socks with dark green tread for grip. "They're the latest style. All the cool kids are wearing these." Why did the nurses take my shoes off?

"The cool kids?" Showing her doubt.

"The coolest! Everyone in the ED has them." As I step on a sharp pebble, biting my tough to not show my pain.

"I'm sure." She giggles as she starts walking up the stairs of the parking complex.

I pause looking at my new arch enemy. "Stairs…" the sound gargled in the back of my throat.

Emily stops at the top of the first flight, realizing my injury is going to be a hindrance. "I bring the car around."

"Are you sure? I can make probably make it."

She say, "Just wait gimpy. I'll be around in a moment." Not wanting to wait on me all day.

Emily bring around a shiny silver Honda Accord. It's not a brand-new car but the paint looks nicer than mine. She makes me put my bag of bloody clothes in the trunk not wanting to risk getting her car messy. I don't point out the piles of empty cups in the back seat. Just smile and do as ask, directing her to apartment complex.

"You really live close. You probably could walk to work."

I look over to the nearest bus stop where a familiar looking street dweller smokes an aluminum foil pipe. "It's not really a walking around kind of neighborhood." I strain to get out of the car. "Thanks for the lift."

"Wait!" Emily grabs me. "Are you sure you're good?"

Still holding onto the car's built in handles I say, "As good as I can be. All things considered."

"Listen, if you need anything. Just text me."

"Are you giving me your number?" Hiding my joy behind shock.

"Yeah, it's no big deal. I'm just worried, you just got stabbed." She see the street dweller as he eats his own skin flakes. "And clearly you're not in the best place."

"I graciously accept." Giving her my number as my phone is still in the trunk. "Text me any time. I will respond if I'm awake."

Sweet, the most beautiful women I know just gave me her number. I am filled with pure joy until I reach the broken stairs to my apartment. "Crap…"

It takes forever to get up the steps. Each time I place down my foot enflames my wound. Eventually I reach the top sweating from the excursion. Oh crap, I don't find my keys in my bag. I'm going to have to go all the way back down the stairs to get the front office to open my door. "Wait a second…" I check the handle, opening the unlocked door. For once I'm glad I don't have anything worth stealing. Besides the blood-stained carpet probably kept people out. My keys are right where I left them on my dresser.

While my phone charges, I take a much-needed hot bath. Keeping my shoulder bandage dry. Scrubbing off the dried blood from my skin. After I listen to a message from Officer James notifying me that Lilith and her boyfriend had skipped town. Before taking a much-needed rest with a locked door.

CHAPTER 24

BORDUM

I LAY IN MY BED FULLY rested, completely lacking the will to move. I've been working nonstop for so long. How do you spend multiple days off? Grocery shopping filled a few minutes yesterday, not that I have a lot of money to spend. I busted out my old Gameboy for a few hours but that barely helps the time pass. The old games don't hit the same anymore.

The only light in these quiet times is when Emily texts to check my condition. I tell her "I'm fine, mostly. It hurts to lift my arm and I can't sleep on my side or stomach. The pain meds prescribed to me have been help a bit."

Emily texts. "Just moved a guy with a stab wound. Maybe you know him."

I replay, "That's Willson. He organizes the yearly meetings."

The conversation continues into a full-on fake lore for us stabbing victims. I could probably turn these text into a book if I had the means to type, How much are computers these days? However her responses become sparser as the day progress with hours passing in between each replay.

Probably a busy day at the hospital, I know for a fact that they are short staffed today.

When I finally beat one of my Gameboy games the silents begins to grow. Listening to the repeating jingle of my old handheld game's soundtrack I feel a desperate need for real sound. My dusty guitar case beckons me toward it. So much time has passed since last I played music, I seriously doubt that any of my skill remain. I could strum a bit of Walt's old songs but with my current injury, can make the chords? Yet I am still pulled to the guitar. Some old feeling dragged up by seeing my old bandmates recently compel. I force myself out of bed to that dusty case. Opening the case my guitar is exactly the way I left it. After tuning the rusty strings I strum a familiar chord. Sending a light pain through my arm, it's not enough to make me stop. Repeating all the old exercises drilled into my head all those years ago I find the range my arm can move without too much pain. I can't go up past the ninth fret. Then the tendons in my hand burn with a familiar strain feeling alive again. I begin playing all the old songs I once knew, opening back up all those memories.

Walt's life journey sown into each of his song. Those warm spring days playing music in his house. I feel him with me as I play. His ghost sings the lyrics that I can't project in my current condition. "You got it boy, keep on strumming!" The rest of the band begins to form back. Tapping my foot to John's mellow drumbeat. "Now take it away." I switch to solo matching Mark's violin melody, while keeping the rhythm with my thumb. The old song morphs into the next one keeping the jam going.

"That really how you want to spend your time, Sebby?" says a pale ghost. As I my hand reaches too high on the guitar which sends a jolt of pain from my should through my body. The song screeches to a stop. As I sit alone once again in my studio apartment. My fingertips throbbing, my calluses long gone from lack of practice.

I retune the old acoustic guitar. Striking a harder chord filled with anger. Playing a song from another past life. Nicolas's old drums erupt as I begin to shred. Bens screams at me as the song begins to rage. My shoulder tenses in pain as Lilith's keyboard matches my melody.

"What kind of crap are you playing now, Sebby?" The pale ghost laughs.

I don't acknowledge him this time. Using my rage to keep play through the pain. Until his laughter is louder than my fingers can handle. As I miss notes as my fingers can't play how they used to.

"You lost your touch."

I shout, "Shut up old man!" immediately collapsing back down holding my burning shoulder.

His laughter fades away as my room returns to silence. I roll flat on the ground with my guitar resting on my stomach. My left arm unmoving against the carpet, reducing all stress on my injury. Slowly picking a melody with my fingers shifting one note from Major to Minor. Creating a constantly shifting sound from positive to stoic. Not a song from my past but of my life now. I'm not sad for I want to live but I'm not happy either. Caught in between, just holding on for the next day. I mumble words that make since. Spinning a tale of a dark place that we must all face someday.

Snap!

The high E string falls limp. I ignore it altering my tune until the high B string snaps. "Damn it…" I return tune to a half step down, loosening the strings. Playing a lower melody of fewer strings. Refusing to stop playing on these old rusty strings until I'm down to my last string the top E string. I switch to a blues pattern of open E to the fit fret of A, open E to A. Capping the pattern on Bm. Even though I know those are not the right notes after the down tune. I rebuild my confidence, knowing my limits to play a more comfortable way.

Hours pass as my fingers are now covered in red rust powder. I don't bother to clean them as I remain on the floor. Just living in the moment for once. I never should have stopped playing.

The next day I hobble into a music store just as it opens. I am immediately overwhelmed by the near one hundred different guitar string types. It has been so long I don't remember what type I use. "Can I get standard Acoustic string." Hoping the employee will know what that means.

"What kind do you like?" The guy not wanting to give a real answer.

"I don't know. What is the average one people buy?"

His glassy red eyes unfocused at the wall of choices. "Well that all depends on what you like best."

This is going nowhere. I see an older gentleman changing string on a guitar at a work bench. "What's the average size for an acoustic guitar strings?"

He doesn't look up from his work. "12-gauge strings. D'Addario are cheap but good. Earnie Ball comes in a pack with three sets." He keeps me from thanking him. "We can replace them for you for twenty bucks. Average return time is three days." He completes his modifications to one guitar moving it to a small, competed pile before taking his next project for a much taller stack of broken guitars.

I buy the pack of three expecting to beak more strings. However, I stop before I leave. To look over the many posters they display for upcoming shows or musician jobs. No bands that I recognize, most the band from my time in the scene have broken up, I guess. There are a bunch of bands looking for bass players and drummers. There always was an abundance of guitarist in this town. One can probably throw a stick at a college campus and hit a guitar player. The only poster that catches my eye is an open mice every Wednesday at a local bar. An old longing creeps back into me. A desire I buried years ago. *I need to perform live.*

CHAPTER 25

LIVE

THE BAR IS EMPTY ASIDE from the bartender. An old familiar feeling makes me wonder if they are even open. I scare her by accident when she notices me standing at the bar. "Sorry, I'm here for the open mice."

Her voice is gravelly from decades of smoking. "You're a bit early darling, the sound guy ain't here yet. Go ahead and choose the time you want to play. Can I get you anything while you wait?"

I almost order a beverage but remember I can't take alcohol while on these pain meds. Then again, I could use a little something to take the edge off. Besides my last dosage should be well within my system. As long as I don't take another pill tonight, I should be good… Probably.

"I'll have a beer."

People slowly fill in as I finish my beer. I am clearly the youngest person here by a considerable amount. Aside from two others, a couple in odd getup. The man is in borderline booty shorts with bright red suspenders. He curls his mustache to complement his muttonchops. While his girlfriend matches with the same shorts but with blue suspenders. Everyone gets three songs. I realized that I signed up for the end of the set. As everyone begins to take the tinny stage, its nothing more than a featureless gray rug no bigger than a doormat. A lady with two long gray braids plays three covers I recognize from the classic rock radio station. Followed by a dude that can't sing a tune in a bucket, as his voice cracks landing nowhere near the key he's playing on guitar. I suddenly feel better as everyone claps for him anyway. The night moves fast aside form a band that takes longer to set up than perform. Eventually Red Suspenders takes the stage just before me with a mandolin unlike the majority of everyone else that used acoustic guitars.

The bar tender gives an enthusiastic cheer, "Welcome back Whisky!"

He takes an Elvis poster, "It's good to be back." As he begins to play an upbeat cover that everyone sings with him. By the second chorus I join with the crowd. Then he sings an original that makes us all laugh. A pit in my gut begins to open as I suddenly realize that I have to follow this. I am nowhere near his level.

The small crowd gives a thunderous applause as Whisky leaves the stage. He says, "Have fun, man."

As I nervously take the stage after him. I give a nervous, "Hi…" to a crowd that could care less for a new face. I can hear that pale ghost laugh at me. My first song is a sloppy attempt to cover one of Walt's classic songs. Missed notes and a voice that hurts to sing too loud completely butchering it. By the time I finish the crowd gives an applause out of obligation.

Somehow indifference feels worse than boos. Now that my hand is warmed up, I play an original from my band. Using attitude to coat the pain. Now the misses matter less as long as I keep the rhythm stable. This time the applause has a real appreciation behind it. However my wound aches from the exertion. So I slow down for my last song. Playing the haunting melody bringing the ghost from the hospital to this small bar. A cold chill radiates from my song causing all other conversations to end. With the final note the applause is slow but bellows into the same thunder Whisky received.

I collapse into the nearest chair from the stage my wound burning. My breath irregular as I stabilize myself.

"Well done!" Says an enthusiastic Whisky taking the empty seat next to me.

"Thanks…" my word genuine but lacking volume.

His girlfriend asks, "You good?"

I show off the bandage on my clavicle. "Fresh stab wound."

She lets out a quiet, "Oh my god."

While Whisky says, "Impressive. And you still took the stage."

"Needed to get out." My breath starting to return to normal.

"I hear that. We do this as often as we can." The couple share a quick kiss. "Tell me are you free in two weeks?"

"Yeah…" Suddenly becoming skeptical. "Why do you ask?"

"There's an event up in Holbrook that I organize performances for. I need another acoustic player my friend had to drop out due to a personal matter. Was planning on asking another friend here but they didn't show up, which is typical of him."

I'm not working from a bit. "Sure why not."

"Awesome, just awesome." Then he asks, "Do you have any kind of apocalyptic costumes?"

"No…" My cut up bloodstained scrubs might count. "Maybe, what kind of event is this?"

"It's a post-apocalyptic festival out in the desert. Think Mad Max mixed with Burning Man but way smaller scale. I took over the entertainment two year ago. I've got a DJ and a suspension show. The standard metal band bailed but we've been leaning toward simpler performances anyway."

"What's a suspension show?"

His girlfriend says, "That's when performers insert hooks into their back flesh and are suspended in the air."

My first thought is *gross*, but instead I say, "Interesting." Seen far worse at the hospital. "I'll do the show as long as I don't have to get suspended."

Whisky laughs at that. "That's only done by the professionals. The event is too far out into nowhere to have armatures get involved. But I think the dude lives around here if I'm not mistaken."

His girlfriend says, "No, Captain Howdy lives in Phoenix but he comes down here for demonstrations."

Wonder if any of his clients have ended up in my Emergency Department. Honestly can't remember anyone with a flesh hook stuck in them. Closest I can think of is a dude with a bunch of nails in his back but that was from a nail gun mishap on a construction site.

Whisky pulls me out of my memories by asking, "Do you have an hour's worth of music?"

I say, "Yea." Out of habit.

"Excellent! And definitely play that last song. That one gave me the chills, in a good way."

Then the realization hits me. I don't have an hour of material. I barely have the three songs. "Does the hour need to be all originals?"

"Nah, most people want to sing along, and popular songs are the easiest way to do that."

Sweet now I have a new goal.

CHAPTER 26

WELCOME TO NOWHERE

"WHERE THE HELL AM I?"

Lost all phone reception twenty minutes ago after I left the freeway. The recommended root pointed me through private property with a sign reading "No trespassing. We are tired of hiding the bodies." On a barbwire gate. Aside from that there is almost nothing for miles. The freeway is just barely still in view along with a few small ranch-like properties, without livestock.

Looking over the hand drawn map Whisky gave me. None of the dirt roads are labeled. I have to guesstimate distance for each odd turn. Hopping that I'm on the right path as I slowly leave behind all of civilization as I crest over a barren hill. At a four-way crossroads I can see for miles with nothing but flat desert in every direction. Not a single plant large enough to provide shade. The sun is bright with very few clouds. I have never been anywhere so open. I'm glad I brought sunscreen.

Thankfully there is a whites van without tires and smashed windows that has Nowhere Springs spraypainted on the side with an arrow pointing north. I've come this far so I keep going avoiding wet spots on this bumpy dirt road.

My car is not designed for mud. I'm at half a tank of gas probably should have filled up before I left the main road.

After an hour of this bumpy dirt road I see a sign at the top of a hill "Nowhere Springs" With a gasmask spraypainted on. In the valley below is a large campsite of makeshift structures of metal and wood. Alongside a few old mobile homes. Driving closer, I can see people working on the structures. My car barely makes it through the dry wash protecting the threshold of this homemade apocalyptic town. There are not nearly as many cars as I anticipated. Whisky made this place sound like a large event of hundreds of people, but there is maybe about fifteen working cars in the parking lot. It is only Friday afternoon, probably won't be really popping until tomorrow night.

At the entrance from the parking lot there are two truck bed campers fused together to form one. A couple is working on something, sounds like hammering wood.

"Hello?"

A man's voice yells out, "Oh…one second."

Followed by a smack and a grunted curse. Out comes a big burly man holding his index finger, followed by a woman half his size. The man ask, "Who are you with?" While the woman thumbs through a clipboard of papers.

"Whisky, I guess. I'm supposed to perform tonight."

The woman hands me a waver to sign, relieving them of all any liability if I hurt myself. She says, "Whisky's camp is at the furthest north point turn right at the fork turning left will take you to the stage. You can park at Whisky's camp tonight, parking lot during the main events to keep everything in theme. What tools did you bring?"

Does she mean camping supplies? "I have a sleeping bag. Was planning on sleeping in my car tonight, and my guitar."

She says, "I see, you're only preforming than." Seeming disappointed in me but smiles when she says, "Looking forward to hearing you."

I drive through the shanty town seeing the many different themed campsites. As people work on their structures. One site has a tiny shed labeled "Postman." Right next to a group of four men digging a large hole, placing the excess dirt into lose tires to form a wall around their pit. While another site is two story tower of wood planks. Held in place with metal cables as the wind sways it back and forth.

I find Whisky clearing dead weeds from his campsite alone. "Glad you made it. Didn't get too lost, did ya?"

"Not too bad. But I thought you said this was a festival. Where is everyone?"

"That's because the festival isn't till next month. This is a build weekend, last chance to get sites ready for the event." He hands me an extra hoe. "Could use an extra pair of hands right now."

I don't take the gardening tool. "Did you just trick me into to driving five fucking hours to do landscaping?"

He sees the disappointment on my face. "Oh, no! Absolutely not. As an untested bard you are trying out in front of the core crowd." Still holding out the gardening utensil for me. "But we don't go on for a few hours and until then I could use some help."

Reluctantly I take the hoe, "I'm already here but don't expect too much I'm still recovering from a stab wound."

While clearing the dead weeds with one arm to not agitate my injury. The wind begins to pick up a good bit. I take the sweaty bandana from my head to protect my face. In this moment of pause many new concerns arise in me. "Hey Whisky!"

Busy fixing his border with the neighboring campsite he asks, "What?"

"Should we be concerned with this wind? Cause those clouds are getting a lot closer." Pointing to the dark storm brewing over the horizon.

He checks the time, "Shouldn't interfere with the performance. I'll talk to the head honcho have us moved to the inside stage."

Then he leaves me alone in as the wind begins to whip more sand into the air. It starts to get so bad I have to retreat to my car as visibility cuts down drastically. A man in a Soviet era uniform appears from the clouds of sand. "Join us for shelter and food." Speaking in a clearly fake Russian accent.

I look at my tiny supply of protein bars and beef jerky. It is not a hard decision. He leads me to their campsite before wondering off to check on other sites. Their structure has tall wooden walls with a sown together tarp roof while pulka plays on an old stereo. The campsite has a Slovak theme with broken props from the cold war as decoration. I take a seat on a fractured car seat masquerading as a couch. I'm given a warm bowl of vegetable and meat soup. I thank them.

The nice lady that made the soup says, "You're new, what brings you to Nowhere?"

"I guess I'm preforming."

Another person in a Slovak outfit says, "Glad to have another bard. But I don't know if you'll be playing tonight. I think the storm is going to hit pretty hard."

The man in the Soviet uniform comes back with more people. Along with Whisky who has my guitar and his mandolin. I forgot to lock my car. He hands me my instrument.

"Main stage is canceled let's just add some background music."

He tells me the root notes of a song than we play a cheery classic as people eat. All while the wind picks up madly whipping the tarp roof about. People join in with us as they recognize the song, and it becomes more of a group shanty. I feel strangely connected to these people I hardly know food and songs bringing everyone together.

A good time until the tarp rips. Sending people into a panic to fix the tear to keep out the sand. While helping to secure the patch rain begins to fall, not a lot of rain it just feels intense because of the wind. The head honcho than grabs everyone's with three loud claps. "Attention! The storm is likely to flood the wash beyond the parking lot tonight. If you do not want to spend the next two day here, I suggest you leave now while you have a chance."

I thank the nice people for the soup and rush to my vehicle. "Whisky, are you coming?"

He says, "Na, I'm good here. Great jam session. I'll see you back here in a month. Just make sure you have a better costume than that."

I look at my work short and wet shirt. Suppose clothing ruined by a painting my parents' house isn't enough for this place. "I'll work on it." Then drive back out of the camp site. Through the sandy wash just as the rain intensifies. At least I made it past the main obstacle but where is everyone else. I can't be the only one leaving. Yet I am the only one on this dark bumpy road.

It was hard enough to drive in here with the sun was up but now I have to do it in reverse, in the dark, all while rain pours down, and sand blows. The dirt is slowly turning into mud. So I maintain a constant slow speed preying that I get back to civilization. Until my vehicle sludges to a stop. I reeve the throttle begging for it to just go one foot further, only to kick up mud. "No! not here damn it!"

I step out my foot sinking into thick muck. I look around for anything that could help. A stick or large rock but there is nothing for miles in this dark desert only dirt turning to mud and dead grass. Thunder illuminates the world for just an instant. I am in the absolute middle of nowhere. The nearest civilization is a ten-mile hike back to the campsite. My phone has no signal and the freeway is miles away. Worse of all I am the only one that decided to leave the campsite. There will be no help moving this car for two days.

"Damnit! I want to go home!" I try to push my car only to get muddier in the process. Then I try to push the car while accelerating only splashing myself and the inside of my car in the process. I yell "FUCK!" as well as a hundred other curse words not all of this material world.

The pale ghost laughs at me. "What are you going to do now Sebby? Wait for rescue."

"I want to go home." Digging my hands into the watery muck behind my tire. "I want to go home!" Scooping out the soupy earth and splashing it to the side. "I'm going HOME!" Then filling the empty gap with dryer dirt from slightly higher ground. I repeat the process for all four of my tires until all the muck is cleared out.

Wet and covered in mud I get back in my car. I accelerate forward unmoving then I slam the breaks and switch to reverse slightly rocking my car. Then repeat the process over and over again until suddenly my car rocks ever so slightly back a foot. "COME ON!" Repeating the process not caring how much time has passed in this dark place beyond the civilized world. Until with one final rock my car rolls free of the mud.

I shout "FREEDOM!" at the top of my lungs laughing like a lunatic ecstatic for this accomplishment.

The Pale ghost does not answer only pointing at my gas gage. I almost used up all my gas to get free. I mutter one rude word, "shit…"

I take the higher ground avoiding the mess I just escaped. Returning to the path back to civilization. Passing familiar homesteads until I reach the freeway as the gas light turns on. "Come on just a little more to go." Nature decided now is a good time to drop the all the remaining rain as I turn onto a busy freeway. Only light is the glorious glow of a large gas station truck stop, "Come on, buddy. We're almost there." Just as I pull off the freeway into salvation my car runs dry. With an anguished groan I get out of the car to push the last hundred yards to the gas pump, as the rain drenches me further. Then as soon as I escape this unwanted shower the rain stops. I look to the sky, "You did that on purpose didn't you."

I can hear the pale ghost laughing.

On the bright side the rain did clean most the mud off the outside of my car. The inside is still a mess as am I. While my tank fills with gas I make my way to the public bathroom to wash what mud that the rain didn't get from myself. Smacking my feet against the curb to knock off the lose mud from my boots. I get strange looks from the truckers as I wash my hands and face in the industrial sized sink.

When I return to my car to clean the windshield, ruining the cleaner for the next person. The inside of my car will need a real clean but that can wait until I get back home. I plug in my phone and put on my heaviest playlist.

The remaining four-hour drive home is completed out of pure spite and anger. As I yell with every song on my playlist on repeat for the entire drive. The rain begins to pour again while the wind picks up.

"Where did all the other cars go?"

The Rain falls harder as the wind intensifies. Visibility suddenly becomes nothing but the yellow line in the middle of the road. I stop yelling with the music only focusing on breathing as the storm intensifies. I would pull off the road if I could see it but the rain is falling hard with strong winds. My windshield wipers are on as high as they can be, I worry that they'll break off. All I can see is that dotted line in the middle of the road every thirty feet, everything else is hidden by the storm. My breathing is deliberate and slow because there is nothing else but my absolute focus on that yellow line.

Then after an hour it clears up, as if nothing happened. The road is empty except for me. Then I see a rest stop completely packed with semitrucks. "So that's where everyone went." With the road to myself I turn the music back up and hit the gas to make up for lost time.

When I finally arrive home at three in the morning. Tripping on the broken step I let out a defeated, "Fuck..." too tired to care. I leave my boots outside my apartment along with my mud-stained clothes that I leave on the railing. Then take the best shower of my life so far. As a layer of dark earth washes off my skin. The bandage over my stab wound falls off finally allowing me to see the wound. It's not as big as I was expecting. In my head I pictured a real long Frankenstein sewing job but it's just a small puncture.

Finally I collapse onto my bed. My phone finally regains a signal and fills with many unread messages. I deal with it all tomorrow as I let the darkness take me.

CHAPTER 27
BACK TO WORK

MY MORNING STRETCHING ROUTINE IS uncomfortably restrictive. The lack of movement my left arm can make is a glaring sign that I'm not fully healed. I think playing guitar may have slowed down the healing process as well. Work is probably going to suck more than normal today. Doesn't help that my only two choices of footwear are in rather bad shape. The hiking boots I took to Nowhere are still caked with mud despite my best efforts to clean them. While my daily shoes that were once comfortable running shoes are stained with my blood. They stopped being white years ago, but the blood stains are rather off-putting. Well if I want to be able to buy some new shoes I'm going to need to go to work.

When I clock in to work, I am immediately assigned morgue run. "Was this one just waiting for me?" I say a bit too cheeky.

Alfred says, "You are the master at these."

"Thanks," I say with a little too much sarcasm.

"Don't worry, I'll have you on light duty after this."

I say, "Thanks," lightly more genuine.

Walking up the hill, that I have not missed, I grumble that I need a new job. Maybe I can transfer to something else at the hospital. Nursing requires a lot more school and I would have to actually care for the patient. No, I've seen what the stress does to them, the money would not be worth it. If I can't afford nursing school than there's no way I can be a doctor. Patient technician might not be bad. The hospital offers free schooling for that path. Then again it would be the same amount of stress as my current job just confined to one unit, with the added bonus of cleaning up excrement.

Maybe I should look into something in the surgery tower. Surgeons need assistance, or cleaning the utensils would probably be on the same level as dishwashing, just more blood.

I find Emily getting the paperwork signed by the acting nurse. She says, "Welcome back was your vacation rejuvenating?"

My mind immediately the thick mud in Nowhere. "Not as much as I would have liked." Quickly wanting to change the subject. "Did I miss anything?"

Emily says, "The usual, patient stuff. There was one patient that died in the lobby. They brought him into the hospital an hour later to declare him dead in the E.D."

Wanting to be a part of the conversation the Nurse says, "I didn't hear about that one. You sure it wasn't the tech that got stabbed by a Crackhead and bled all over the E.D lobby?"

Emily gives me a knowing look. "No, I heard that was a separate incident."

In the morgue Emily does most the heavy lifting. While operating the wall forklift, I ask, "How many different roamers are there about me?"

"There were a lot the first day." Emily jokes, "My favorite was that you fell trying to do a handstand." While pulling out a fresh chart.

"I almost bleed to death in the lobby and everyone is making jokes."

"Don't be so shocked. Like you said dark humor gets us through the day here. Besides you had to know there would be rumors. You walked through the halls in bloody scrubs. Even the people who had the day off knew a transporter got stabbed. And without you around theories spread like wildfire." Emily says as she pushes fresh body into the fridge.

After locking the big metal door shut. I swear The Pale Ghost is right behind her winking at me but as soon as I blink, he's gone. Emily looks around, "Are you good for today?" suspecting that I saw something.

"As good as I can be."

"Can I ask you something?" Her eyes wide with worry.

My heart pumps a little faster as I begin to burn hot. "Of course…"

Shaking with fear Emily asks, "Do you ever see things around here, that aren't exactly there?"

Dark black eyes peak at me from the shadows. All the heat leaves my body replaced with a cold chill. I gently nudge Emily out of this creepy room before answering. In the bright Buck hall I say, "All the time."

"Really?" Relieved she says, "I thought I was just going crazy."

"Oh, no you are. But so am I."

She nudges me playfully. "Jerk."

"But seriously though. This place has got to be haunted. You hear stories of ghosts haunting where they died and where do people die the most."

"Right here in the ICU." Emily says discouragingly

"So they probably linger. The funny thing is I've only ever heard about ghost in scary stories, but it's just kind of a nuisance."

"To you maybe. I keep hearing crying when I'm alone. It's freaken me out!" Emily shutters with frustration.

"Oh, that's just me. I run away before you can see."

She glares at me, but I can see a little smile at the edge of her mask. "You're the worst." Before letting out a small giggle. "I need a new job."

"We both do." Agreeing before finally closing out the morgue run and going our separate ways for the shift. My day becomes primarily specimen runs. Various bits of people to be delivered to the lab. Easy to do with one good arm. Got stuck in the elevator for ten minutes after delivering drugs to third floor Pre-opt. For once I don't mind the delay as I sit in the enclosed space staring at my blurred reflection in the metal doors. Just to watch my refection shift my skin to pale white and my eyes darken.

"You're still a loser. A young women looked to you for guidance and all you could do was crack jokes."

"I know." Is the only answer I can give.

CHAPTER 28
THE CURRENT SCENE

IT'S SATURDAY AND I'M NOT working. This is a strange feeling. Kind of like I should do something, but I have no idea what. I've always worked Saturday, that's just how it's almost always been. Most people prefer to have today off, so people like me that have zero social life work. Now after my injury my schedule has been shifted. Been too coopted up resting, so I should go out but where?

Could hit up Nick maybe meet his fiancé.

Turns out they're busy planning a wedding.

What other friends do I even have? Definitely not going to reach out to Lilith. I don't need another near fatal injury or broken heart.

"You know what, I'll go to my old stomping grounds." That bar always had live music Saturday nights. Even for the small crowds. In an old local band shirt I make the trek to the terrible parking on the edge of Downtown. The Stumble Inn was a solid venue for local bands to take a medium stage. National touring acts will sometimes book here. Primarily for weekday shows that can't fill a larger theater. That never mattered to me, I used to love the live shows.

That comfortable nostalgia leaves a soon as I step out of the car to pay for parking. Remembering my last gig here, when Ben couldn't play straight and puked all over this very same pay box. Ben made every single show stressful. If we played early in the lineup, he would be late, maybe making it on time. If we played late, he would be completely plastered and be unable to play the songs right.

The Stumble Inn is currently doing a battle of the bands. The person at the door ask, "Which band are you here for?"

"All."

"Well just put your ticket the box for the band you like best."

The first band starts blasting with a loud unintelligible screech that hurts my ears. I immediately regret not bringing earplugs. My ears can't handle a full night of this. Can't leave the venue without having to pay for reentry, so I go to the men's restroom. In the far back corner of the venue without entry door. The long sink urinal is still marked with chewing tobacco stains. The once black and white tiled walls are now completely covered in band stickers. Thankfully the only sit down is empty. I can tell because the saloon doors leave a noticeable gap in between. Of course when I step in my foot makes a very district sticking sound, sending an aggravated shiver down my spine. It's not a fresh stick but I know it can't be good. I don't look down, won't do any good now. All I do is rip off a few pieces of toilet paper roll them into two small balls and pack them into my ears.

I can't hear the residual sticking of my shoe anymore, but I can still feel it. At least now the venue's volume no longer hurts my ears. Now I can safely hear this band sound like absolute crap. The bass is completely off of the drums and the guitarist keeps missing notes. While the lead singer, no that's not the right term. The front screamer has yet to say any words in key. This is just angry noise. With their audience being about three people, a relative, a girlfriend, and me. The other bands aren't even giving these guys the time of day.

When their set finally ends, I am relieved to have a moment of silence. While the next band gets ready. The crowd grows by a total of ten. One of the other bands came in but keep to themselves in their merch corner.

The next band begins and there is a noticeable improvement. They all play on time and most of the vocals are legible. The guitar solos are a tad long but other than that a solid listening experience. A few people even start to mosh a bit. I back away not wanting to get sucked in. Then I feel someone grab my shoulder. I feel as though something is being shouted at me, but I can't hear them over the music. I turn to look what's up expecting it to be a bouncer. Instead I see an old friend with rage in his eyes.

"Ben?"

Pow! His fist meets my face. The shock knocks me off balance, but I don't drop. I've been hit much harder by old men in the hospital. Another fist flies at me. I try to weave for my standard dodge, but Ben holds tight to throw another punch striking my forehead this time. Ben had always been thin one shove throws him off. As I brace for another onslaught, we are both grabbed by much larger men and physically thrown from the establishment.

Both of us tumble onto the sidewalk, Ben starts yelling at me before either of us are back to our feet. "You got some fucking nerve coming to my show you, traitor!" Swaying an as he is clearly inebriated.

Popping back to my feet, "I didn't even know you were playing! You prick."

The rest of his band comes out one man with an excessive amount of eye liner says, "Damn it, Ben! We just got kicked off the bill. What did you do. You know what no, I don't care. You're out we'll get a new bass player." He turns to another man with far less eyeliner. "Darick see if Soul Harvesters is willing to lend their bass player tonight. I'll beg Kent to let us back on the bill."

Ben protests, "Wait! I'm still good to jam."

"I don't care! You are not costing us another gig."

"Please Nate." The desperation in Ben's voice breaking through.

They all turn their backs to us to reenter the establishment as security creates a door blocking us.

Ben turns back to me. "Look what you did!"

"What I did? You attacked me, unprovoked!"

"Maybe if you didn't abandon the band this would never have happened!"

A possibility flashes through my head if I had never of tried for the police academy. This time unobstructed by nostalgia. After Nicholas and Lilith's brutal break up. The band would have just been the three of us Nicholas, Ben and I. Nicholas would have still gone down the same academic path, leaving us for a real career. Ben would have continued to get drunk at every opportunity as I carried the band. As we played empty bars for no pay. I would be in the same position I am now but with the weight of a shitty band on my shoulders.

The thought is quick only a fraction of a second, but I still see it clear as day. "No… I made the correct choice. Ben you are an addict pushing the responsibility for you actions on to me."

"We could have made it if not for you." Striking back with his old tried and true accusation. I had to block his number because of all the messages he left me saying just that.

"No one was looking for us! How do you not understand that. This isn't the nineties anymore. Record labels don't send out agents to find the next big thing. A band has to already be successful before they even consider offering a contract to own their music. Do you even remember our largest audience size because I do. I was sober!" Ben tries to say something, but I cut him off. "Ten people! And half of that was the other members of the bands. Our band sucked! Sorry to burst your bubble but you can't hold a tune in a bucket with your smoke-filled lungs."

Ben just sits there a moment still on the ground. Unable to process his reality shattering. I almost feel bad, that I offer him a hand up. "Come on."

He doesn't take it. Just stares in horror behind me. Enough so that I turn around to see what could possibly be behind me. Then all the blood leaves my face as the world around us freezes. My eye meet Lilith's then her much larger boyfriends, then back to her in quick succession. As my heart begins to pound. No words are spoken as only one action is taken.

Run!

Ben grabs my hand in desperate move to stand up faster. Shifting me off balance, but not enough to stop me. We both start sprinting at full speed. As the adrenaline has fully kicked it. The only thought is to get as far away as possible. Can't tell if we are being chased. The feeling of someone's fingers almost grabbing the back of my neck pushes me forward.

My car isn't too far. Pulling the electronic key from my pocket I being pressing the unlock button in desperation causing it to beep multiple times. As fast as I can I open the car door and slam it behind me. Then as I put the key into the ignition Ben slides over the hood with the grace of an inebriated cat followed quickly by a gorilla of a man diving after him. Ben lands on his feet and jump into my car before Lilith's boyfriend can turn around. I slam on the ignition driving over the curb for a quick escape.

Only to screech to a stop at a red light for a busy intersection.

Sucking air Ben looks back, "They're still coming!"

Come on light give us the green already. I can see two shadows running up the street at us. The light changes just before they reach us, and I speed out of downtown.

The car is silent while we both catch our breath. I kind of chuckle while Ben does the same until we both start to laugh uncontrollably. We laugh for at least a mile before we start to calm down. I don't need to ask why he was running from them; I already know.

Ben calms down first, "You put your dick in crazy didn't you."

"To be fair I didn't know she was that crazy." Trying to defend my stupid actions.

Ben still call, "Bullshit, you saw her lose it on Nicholas."

"Says the guy who jumped in her pants first opportunity he got. Wait did you invite her to your show tonight?"

"Well, yeah. I heard she had broken up with her boyfriend."

"You heard wrong. She hadn't broken up with that goliath. I bailed her out of the crazy house, and she stabbed me."

"You picked her up from an asylum."

I correct him, "Crisis Response Center."

He continues, "Bail her out of an Insane asylum and still thought it's a good idea to put your dick in her? You're dumber than me."

I chuckle, "Now that's saying something."

Ben smiles at that as I laugh a little bit more.

I take Ben back to his place, which isn't far from my apartment complex. When he gets out, he says, "I'm sorry about hitting you tonight."

"I'm good, didn't hurt. You're still built like a string been."

He signs not wanting to argue. "Listen if you ever want to just jam sometime…"

Seeing were this is going I say, "I'll consider it only if you promise there is no bullshit this time around, just the music."

Ben says, "I promise." before getting out of my car and walking into an even worse looking apartment complex.

CHAPTER 29

BACK TO NOWHERE

I CAN'T BELIEVE I'M DOING THIS again. Driving back into desert nowhere land. Bumping right past the dried mud patch with tire track frozen into a permanent part of the road. On the bright side the land scape looks slightly lusher after the heavy rainfall.

This time when I crest over the hill Nowhere is a bustling village. The parking lot is packed with cars. People have been here all week enjoying the festival. This is technically the last day with clean up tomorrow. Kind of wish I could have seen the other days. Gonna have to rebuild my time off after my forced month of recovery. This time when I sign the waver I am told to remain in costume at all times. "It's for the décor of the event." Makes since if you paid to go to an apocalypse cosplay event on this scale. Seeing someone one in plain clothes would be disappointing.

In the parking lot I put on my resewn blood-stained scrubs with my mud ruined boots. As well as a healthy layer of sunscreen. With my camping pack on and guitar case in hand I enter the Nowhere festival grounds. Taking the scenic route to Whiskey's camp site. I want to take in the event with all the colorful people. Lots of fun costumes reminiscent of Mad Max. Along with some unique takes, my favorite so far is a post apocalypse Charlie Chaplin, the dude is doing everything in character. When I pass the big hole next to the post office, there are a half dozen people sharing a pipe that smells distinctly like a skunk. A dude in a barbarian leathers offers me the pipe. I politely decline, I'm willing to bet money my work is going to drug test me when I get back. The Slovik camp has some old military surplus for sale. I might have to buy one of those canteens.

Whisky is napping in the shade when I arrive at the campsite. I don't bother to wake him, setting up my tent for the night. However when I take a bite out of my super sandwich he wakes up. "What the heck is that?"

"This is my meal for the weekend." I show off the great creation. "Swiss, lettuce, turkey, pesto, and olives, in one uncut bread loaf. Ain't got to worry about cooking this time."

He says, "Smart." Readjusting his hat to return to his nap. "We go on at seven just as the sun sets."

Leaving Whisky to nap I wonder the town. My current priority is figuring out the bathroom situation. Not surprised there's no plumbing out here. The only option are protopodites are made out of building scraps, with a toilet seat attached to a large plastic barrel. There are instructions stating to put in a scoop of sawdust after each use. At least they supplied toilet paper. It's fine until one of the many flies attempts to go up my nose. Forcing me to smack my face, squishing the insect in my nostril. I blow out the mushed chunks, but it still feels like something is lodged in there, even though I've cleared out all of the debris.

Wondering the town I find my way to the Main Street. The row of shacks are now little shops with items of the apocalypse. I purchase a ruined bardic hat with a burned feather. Then the dude working the fabric shop calls me over. "This is your first event isn't it. That's a nice attempt, but you need something more." He takes out a green military jacket from the seventies. "This will complete the costume, fifteen bucks."

I say, "It's a bit hot for a jacket."

"Trust me it will get real cold tonight. By the way what did you use for the fake blood?"

I buy the jacket. "It's not fake. All mine."

He laughs at that. "Good one."

When the first cold breeze arrives with the setting sun, I am glad to have the old jacket. Definitely needs a wash though.

The stage is welded metal designed to look broken and rusty. Upon close inspection it's clear that it will not fall apart just yet. Even though the tires stacks surrounding the sharp edges are definitely unstable. Whiskey works to clear the dust build ups from the mixing board. It takes him an hour before the we can get sound working, "You're lucky you only have the guitar. The metal band last night took even longer for sound check. Dude had two bass drums instead of just a double bass pedal, that's just excessive."

With sound all set I take the stage. The main street is still light enough to see the town and into the vast desert. I feel nervous but not scared. My first strum of the guitar causes intense feedback forcing Whisky to kill the power. After a readjustment I try again. Playing an old classic to warm up. People wonder over as the desert grows dark. I play Walt's legacy bringing in more people. However this time I play the haunting song of the Hospital before the fun upbeat stuff. Summoning the ghosts of this desolate land. As I finish the song, Whiskey triggers a torch behind me that lights up the area with a flash of light. I end my short set with a few happier songs and a familiar pop song that people join in with my singing.

My set is passable as I am cheered for my performance. However, they all cheer for Whisky as soon as he takes the stage. His songs are far better than mine, I'm glad I'm not playing after him. While Whisky plays a group in the audience congratulates me and ask, "What's your name."

I say, "Sebatian."

"No not your name from the world. Your apocalypse name."

There's only one that comes to mind, "The Last Responder."

After Whisky plays the flesh suspension people set up in front of the stage. With hooks already in their back meat. They are lifted into the air moving to a twisted melody. A mesmerizing display, without a drop of blood.

The final performance for the night is a magician with seven burlesque dancers. He does not do any simple card tricks. No, this sorcerer does grand escapes demonstrating his power. Makes my simple acoustic performance seems kind of lame in comparison.

Upon completion of the performance people wonder off for the night life. Drinks of booze are sold out of a broken school bus. While people gamble for bottle caps, no old-world money allowed. All the caps I win at blackjack, I lose at Craps. So I find an nearby fire pit where people are eating pizza. They invite me over with a slice. The mushrooms are a tad dray but overall not bad. Nice change from my Super sandwich currently sitting in my pocket.

They laugh and wonder off. Then a man with white hair sits next to me. "Fuck this place." He grumbles.

I say, "It's not bad, there's food and fire."

"All my friends are ignoring me. Completely written me off."

Why is he telling me this? I don't know you. "I'm sorry, dude."

He turns to me, "It's ok though because I'm a killer."

Oh, shit… I slowly take my hands out of my pockets. Don't need to get stabbed again.

"I spent ten years in the NSA erasing people."

I turn my body to face him, trying to control my racing heartbeat.

"We need another player for blackjack!" Shouts a dis-embodied voice.

My hand shoots up. "I'll join!" As I quickly back away.

A large man in a bright red duster deals me in. He says, "Stay away from that guy."

"Thanks, I don't need another stab wound."

The man in read gestures to a guy with ancient ruins tattooed to his face. "Commotion, keep an eye on Crowly, he's making threats again."

The tattooed man disappears into the night shadowing my would-be attacker.

Slowly the card begin to warp in my hands. What the hell? My grip becomes loose as all the cards fall. "Those weren't normal mushrooms on that pizza where they?"

The big man in red says, "You had some of that pizza. Buckle up dude, you're about to go on a trip."

I leave the table.

"Do you need help getting back to your camp?" asks another man at the table with a long dark beard and a brand on his neck.

"No… I should be fine."

However when I walk away from the light, I enter the spirit world.

CHAPTER 30
THE PALE GHOST

THE SHADOWS OF THE PAST encircle me. As the twinkling star light bounces off the desert sand. Forgotten past lives shine down upon me. Faceless spirits from an older world encircle me except for one. One ghost stands before me. One that refuses to leave me alone. His unmistakable face never smiles even when he would laugh. "Did you really let a bunch of hippies drug you."

"I was hungry."

"Not the right answer, moron. You never knew how to make the right choices. Even when they were right in front of you."

"I made the best choices I could."

"And they were always wrong. You miserable excuse for a man."

We are alone in the spirit world the shadow of all else long faded away.

His barrel chest out he accuses me, "Of lacking ambition."

I turn to leave only to see him still in front of me. There is no escaping him now.

"You've failed at everything you ever attempted. You couldn't get a date in college. You failed to get into the Police academy. You chased after Kelly like a lovesick puppy. And worst of all you let Lilith stab you. How could a such a pathetic loser even share a drop of my blood. I married at twenty-two, and proudly served on the force for thirty years while raising four kids."

Each word cuts a wound deep inside me. I failed to live up to what he set before me.

"You are a pathetic excuse for a grandson."

I have no excuses but, "I did my best."

"No you didn't. If you had than you would have cheated on the colorblind test."

"I didn't know I was color blind."

"And you didn't think to lie. It doesn't take a genius to figure that one out."

"Then what?" Finally talking back. "What would I have done then? Passed and screwed over some pour bystander because I can't tell the difference between a blue car and a purple car."

He doesn't back down. "If it were me."

I cut him off. "It wasn't you. I'm not you!" My words feeling true. "I am not you grandpa. You had your life. It ended ten years ago. I'm doing the best I can with what I have but it's not the same world you knew. Back in your day you could get away with being colorblind. I can't and I didn't jeopardize my values to get here. Yeah, it sucks that I can't do what my life was dedicated to but I'm glad I was able to be with Walt in his final moments. I'm happy to be out here playing music with these hippies. You never left your hometown. You never saw anything like this in your time. True it hasn't worked out how I planned but that ain't a bad thing."

He says, "You're still a lonely loser."

"I'm ok with that. You couldn't handle being alone with your own thoughts. That's why you completely shut down when grandma died. I can and someday I know I will find someone who will care for me the same way I care for them."

"Is that right Sebby?"

"Yes! It is."

He smile, "Then you don't need me anymore." Fading away into the darkness of the spirit world.

While I wake up in the empty desert without the campsite nowhere to be seen. "Crap…" My head hurts. The sun crest over the horizon illuminating the distinct lack of civilization in every direction.

"Ok… don't panic. Where is my sandwich?" Noticing the scattered pieces around me.

I walk to the top of the nearest hill hoping to get a better view of the land. Hoping I didn't wonder too deep into nothing without water. Thankfully at the top of the hill I find the Nowhere campsite just in the valley below. As well as my shirt caught in the brush. After a brush off I return to my campsite to pack up.

Whiskey hears me and stumbles from his tent. "Hey, sorry I couldn't find you last night. Great show, you are welcome back anytime."

"Thanks, it was nothing compared to your set. Or the fucking sorcerer."

"Don't feel bad. Nothing is as good as him out here." Then he falls right back into his tent.

The drive home is much easier this time now that I'm in a convoy with many others leaving the campsite. Then upon arriving back home I shower off a layer of dust, just to get ready to return to work tomorrow.

CHAPTER 31

LIFE DOESN'T STOP

I CLOCK IN AND COLLECT MY Voicera. My phone lights up with my first job, morgue run in 413. It's my patient from yesterday. Giving me a sick feeling in my gut. Today however there are too few transporters to lend assistance. So I'm moving this limp body bag on my own. The night nurse bailed as soon as she signed the paperwork. The only person willing to help is a janitor mopping up the next unit over.

The morgue is packed with bodies. Clearly a busy weekend. After a game of body Tetris I get the latest corpse into the fridge. It's just another body, just another day of work.

The day passes by as I move beds with bodies from one end of the hospital to the other. I place my mind on the Nowhere festival. How did that sorcerer pull off some of those tricks? That distraction only last so long before reality brings me back to the hospital. Moving a patient with a nasty head wound, I can't take my eyes off the gash.

I hate this place.

Then I see her at the far end of the hallway. Emily is walking to get a patient, the light of the rising sun reflecting perfectly off of her golden hair. It's only for a moment as she enters the nine hundreds unit. For a moment my heart flutters in a way I didn't know it could in this place. Do I like Emily? She was the only one to text me while I was on bed rest. I wonder if she has any feeling for me. She wouldn't have given me her number if she didn't care at least a little bit.

She's the only thing on my mind as I move patients. I need to talk to her, but she's always just out of reach. Either I'm pushing a patient and she's entering a unit or she's with a patient while I'm transporting blood. I'm never in the right place at the right time. I'm actually hoping for another morgue run or an oversized patient, because than I might get her as a partner. Unfortunately, the day goes by smoothly without any really difficult jobs.

When the shift ends, I turn in all my paperwork, twenty-five jobs in total, not bad. While counting another transporter is turning in their paperwork as well. Without looking up I ask, "How many did you get?"

Emily says, "twenty-six."

"Emily! Hey, what are you doing after work? What to get some coffee with me?" The words shooting out of me without an ounce of thought.

There is a moment of awkwardness as Tony the dis-patcher turns away to avoid getting involved.

Emily breaks the silence, "I don't really like coffee."

"Tea?" My hope draining.

She shrugs, "Sure, why not."

We clock out together talking about all the crazy pa-tients we got during our shift today. She apparently had a violence risk patient take a swing at her. She demonstrates her dodge. An efficient movement of grace.

At the top of the parking garage I look out at the hospital with the sun at my back. This has been the craziest few months of my life. I've moved at least a hundred bodies to the morgue. I lost my virginity and was stabbed by the same woman. The man that taught me to play guitar died. I also played my first solo show out in literally Nowhere. And a patient died in my care.

Emily asks, "Are you alright?"

"Yeah, the hospital looks oddly quiet from here."

She lights up, "But we know the truth."

"Yes, we do."

Dear Reader,

Thank you for taking the time to read this story. I plan to keep telling stories for as long as I'm alive. This one in particular is close to me for it very much is my story. I wrote this as a bit of therapy to process my time as a Medical Transporter, as well as my failed dating experiences. Some things were changed to make this a more exciting and faster story for you, and all the names of people I worked with were changed for the sake of privacy. The biggest change was the ending—I left the hospital for a better job opportunity and the woman Emily is based off of actually was not interested in me. That's the nice thing about fiction, being able to give Sebastian the happy ending I never had.

I wish everyone I worked with at the hospital the best and hope they are doing well wherever they are now.

—Matt Simons

ABOUT THE AUTHOR

A man with a sense of humor that does not exclude himself, Matt Simons is known among friends and family by his nickname, Nightstand, which he earned while carrying a nightstand down three flights of stairs and across two blocks before realizing it was nearly killing him because it was full of weights. The heavy lesson learned: check the contents of what you will carry around before lifting it.

Let's connect on social media!

Instagram: https://www.instagram.com/nightstand_matt/

Bluesky: @nightstandmatt.bsky.social